W. Watman Smith

Village Life and Sketches

With Other Poems

W. Watman Smith

Village Life and Sketches
With Other Poems

ISBN/EAN: 9783337158484

Printed in Europe, USA, Canada, Australia, Japan

Cover: Foto ©Andreas Hilbeck / pixelio.de

More available books at **www.hansebooks.com**

VILLAGE LIFE

AND

SKETCHES.

With other Poems.

BY

W. WATMAN SMITH.

INDEX.

PREFACE.

———

ONLY a limited number of this little offspring of the Muses has been printed for private distribution amongst friends, who are known to possess some poetical taste in this prosaic age of politics and business.

The principal poem, ' Village Life and Sketches'. is a superficial attempt to picture a few features of humble life, as well as to sketch the leading characters of note in this primitive village ; glancing by the way at some of the customs and amusements of its inhabitants, as well as the sports and pastimes of country life.

Writing at intervals, to beguile a leisure hour in the sunset of life, and cherishing a fondness for retirement from the busy haunts of men, with a natural love for rural scenery, amidst the choir of joyous birds revelling in summer sunshine, I found pleasure in depicting the flowery landscape and rustic employments of pastoral and agricultural life.

It is not for a moment conceived that the gay and pleasure seeking world would find much interest in the dull monotony of the country; or that the novelist who has a voracious appetite for the sensational, would have patience to wade through a book which contained no story or plot to stimulate his heated fancy in conjuring up fresh scenes and incidents in every chapter of his novel.

Much as the works of art interest and elevate the inquiring mind, and scientific discoveries enlarge our knowledge in increasing the comforts and diminishing the wants of life, yet the gigantic works of nature absorb in glorious contemplation the works of Creation, inspiring profound reverence for the Creator, who out of chaos wrought the firmament of Heaven, in which our planet is dimly visible.

'Helicon' is but a dream of the imagination. On the sacred seat of the Muses the immortal souls of the poets are supposed to be pining in mental suffering, doing penance for their earthly sins, before ascending to the regions of bliss, to join their symphonies with the seraphs and cherubim of light, who surround the throne of the Eternal.

The 'Epistle' and minor poems call for no special comment, being the spontaneous productions of idle time, whose characteristics will be found in their titles, which indicate the subject, and must be judged of by their truthfulness to nature and lyrical harmony.

VILLAGE LIFE AND SKETCHES.

PART I

HAIL, joyous May! sweet sister month of Spring,
Whose glorious advent heralds came to sing,
With bursts of sunshine, when the cloister'd sun
Breaks through the veil of clouds that environ.
The wand of magic changed the winter gloom
To cheerful smiles which soften and illume;
The death-struck trees revive, shoot forth and bud,
Reanimated with their vital blood,
And over them a radiant, rapturous glow
Of warmth and feeling quickens as they grow,
Till an exuberant foliage of green,
Clothes every branch and renovates the scene.
The face of heaven wears one continual smile
Of gladdening sunshine round this fairy isle,

B

And simple spring-flowers decorate the earth
That teems and swells in giving them their birth.
The early primrose, modest, meek and shy,
In shady woodlands first attracts the eye;
The pendent snowdrop, and the glen's blue bell,
The violet of aromatic smell,
And the mezereon with her bashful leers,
And the sweet almond ere a leaf appears:
The clustering peach tree as it climbs the wall,
And wallflowers scatter their perfume o'er all.
The yellow blazing furze next glads the sight,
And gold laburnum, graceful, glowing, bright,
With drooping lilac scatt'ring rich perfume,
And chesnut with its pyramids of bloom,
The scented thorn, and flowers of every hue,
With other floral beauties Spring renew!
The unfledged nestlings chirp aloud for food,
The anxious mother feeds her tiny brood,
The friendly robin sings his sprightly lay,
And mavis carols through the gladsome day;
On wings of liberty outspread they fly
Midway between the ocean, earth, and sky;
E'en as the bird from out his covert sings,
So from my rustic bower my idyl springs.

The quiet hamlet to a village grows,
The village to a town, and overflows
With population like a hive of bees,
When myriads emigrate and cross the seas
To lands of promise, prompted by foresight,
Like birds of passage ere they take their flight ;
Opening new colonies in isles remote,
Which by degrees advance to fame and note,
Retired and snug in its own circling arms,
By distant hills surrounded, and the charms
Of rural scenery, the Village stands,
Where yon square tower o'erlooks the fruitful lands.

Still-life runs through it, but the open green
Presents a gay and animated scene ;
Its pristine character, medieval look,
Time honour'd history,—meandering brook,
Its ancient hall, its market place, and inn,
Noted for comfort and good cheer within ;
With some new buildings at the western end,
And rustic scenery round, an int'rest lend.
A long wide straggling street runs winding through,
Presenting illustrations to the view

Of humble life diversified with shops,
Where the fond gaze of admiration stops
The gaudy maiden or the rustic clown:
It bears the semblance of a rising town,
Enliven'd with the bustling passers by,
And hucksters' carts and wagons of supply.
Without design or any general plan,
Rude chaos reign'd, and wild disorder ran;
Private with public residences rise,
A heterogeneous mass in shape and size;
A creeping honeysuckle, vine or rose,
Spreads out its arms and o'er the cottage grows;
And here and there a damsel at the door
Sings o'er her crochet needle by the hour.
Hark! in the distance, on the breezes borne,
Is heard the sound of bugle or of horn,
As the stage-coach comes dashing through the street,
When eager eyes at doors and windows meet,
Creating stir and bustle at the 'Vine,'
Where passengers alight to drink or dine.
The Quarter sessions of the neighbouring town,
Thinn'd off the vagabonds and kept crime down.
The weekly market held throughout the year,
Attracted farmers' wives and tradesmen here,
Tempting the dainty palate with good cheer.

The smoky smithy lazy loungers found,

Where gossip, scandal, and the news went round ;

Here an old raven hopp'd and jump'd about,

And teazed would threat to pluck their eyeballs out ;

The wandering gipsies fix their tented camps,

While locomotive pedlars, hucksters, tramps,

Impart vitality and give a tone

Of quiet trading to the sleepy town.

Pragmatic Punch raised his shrill mimic voice,

Whose fun and drollery made the swains rejoice.

The organ grinder with his sun-tann'd face,

And dancing monkey cheer'd the lifeless place ;

While over all a settled peaceful calm

Of social friendship adds a double charm,

Where pride and vanity were little known,

But mutual courtesy to all was shown.

Their fathers long before had settled here,

And lived contented in their pristine sphere ;

A stagnant race ! few rose to wealth or fame,

As in the beginning, they remain the same.

An agricultural district smiles around,

No staple manufacture it renown'd,

Nor rumbling railroads yet disturb'd its calm,

With clouds of smoke and shrieks of false alarm,

Tainting the atmosphere so sweet and clear,
Which gives a healthy hue throughout the year.

At break of day comes stealing into town,
All veil'd with dew and covered o'er with down,
The creeping wagon with its jingling bells,
And crackling whip the lazy team impels ;
The dreaming driver in smock-frock attired,
With his 'good morning,' drowsy looks and tired,
The old post chaise (now almost obsolete)
Attracted all as it rush'd through the street.
The ruddy milkmaid up at early dawn,
Awakes with music's voice the blushing morn,
As with quick step she plies her simple trade,
Fresh from the dairy to the sluggish maid ;
Then sings her way across the rustic stile,
With graceful briskness and good temper'd smile.
The little birder with his bait and call,
Entangles in his net the captive small,
Who unsuspicious falls into the snare,
Which cunning art and cruelty prepare.

One pretty custom, pleasing and polite,
Inspires goodwill and gratifies the sight,

When lads and lasses their good manners shew,
By dropping a low curtsey or a bow,
To those above them in the social scale,
A feudal custom which may long prevail !
The village gossips would their scandal talk
In groups assembled, or their shopping walk,
And prate of good home-brew'd or elder wine,
Dress, local news, and weather rough or fine.

At early dawn the notes of chanticleer,
From his expanded throat burst shrill and clear,
Breaking the solemn stillness of the night,
Ere the sun rises with his beams of light,
Waking the slumbering tenants of the wood
To vocal harmony and chirping brood,
Till blazing out the sun begins to rise,
Filling with song-birds the illumined skies,
The friendly robin's note from dell or lane,
Is to the weather-wise a sign of rain.
When jet black crows are hovering around
Their lofty eyries with a Babel sound,
And early ploughmen drive their team afield,
Or harvest corn crops to the sickle yield,

While to the farmyard, which is all astir,
Some wend their way with 'a fine morning, sir.'

The farmhouse maid attends the milching cow,
The husbandmen the harrow and the plough.
The drover with his bleating flock and herd,
Gives the trained dog the magic sign or word,
Who scours the field swift as an arrow's flight,
Startling the timid sheep with bark and bite,
And drives the stragglers into fold and place,
As o'er their backs he leaps and runs a race;
The shepherds hurdle in their flocks and herds,
Charmed with the dulcet notes of singing birds.

The western hills had welcomed in the Sun,
And o'er the sky its misty veil was spun,
The tints of crimson in the west are spread,
The busy sounds of industry have fled,
The lofty trees their spreading branches rear,
And their thick foliage darkens all the air;
A dim cathedral light falls through from heaven,
Softly retreating 'fore the shades of even,
And smiling Venus rises in the sky,
Opening the curtain of her brilliant eye,

As on his fiery wings recedes afar,

The imperial god of planet, moon, and star.

The lingering twilight lit the shady dells,

While blending voices of the village bells,

Like merry gleemen chimed across the lea,

Borne by the gales which kiss'd from every tree,

O'er which their fluttering wings expanded flew,

Its sweet exhaling breath and silver dew.

The blackbird's whistle from the thicket sprung,

The woodlands echoed and the mountains sung,

A dying groan is uttered by the oak,

As it descends before the woodman's stroke.

The winding paths of yon secluded spot,

Descending reach the woodman's low-built cot:

Yon curling smoke discovers through the trees

The straw-thatch'd cottage shelter'd from the breeze.

Here all his pleasure, all his soul's desire,

Sits smiling round him by his faggot fire,

His industry their daily wants supply,

And sweet contentment glistens in his eye.

The cawing rook seal'd up its prattling tongue,

When evening's mantle round its eyelids hung ;

The brook meandering at the meadow's feet,

Went slowly rippling to its still retreat,

Its pensive voice resembling human sighs,
When in distress petitioning the skies;
The patient angler casts his baited line,
And hooks the fish that knew not his design;
The lowing kine were straggling into view,
Along the green lane where the hawthorn grew;
The shepherd's dog was at his master's heels,
As he went whistling homeward through the fields;
The scaring crow-boy who the cornfields beat,
And sounds the sooty foragers' retreat,
With his war rattle climbing o'er the stile,
Departs the scenes of his accustomed toil;
The weary ploughman mantled in his frock,
Guiding the ploughshare hears the village clock,
Whose mellow tones float on the viewless gale,
Like infant voices which a parent hail:
The cheering sound vibrates upon his ear,
As he departs to meet his children dear.
The joys that wait him at his blest abode,
He fancies to himself upon the road,
Short'ning his journey as he drives his team,
With 'Home, sweet home,' the burden of his dream:
With bright'ning face he sees (oh! happy state)
His buxom partner at the garden gate,

The binding pledges of their nuptial bliss,
Half naked run to share the hearty kiss,
Their prattle falls like music on his ear,
As they rehearse in broken accents clear,
With frequent bursts of laughter to prolong,
The news and gossip of the village throng;
Their childhood gambols and their school complaints,
With artless innocence the urchin paints.
Inheriting his likeness, they all share
His hale complexion and familiar air.
Their lineaments were like, and you might trace
The father or the mother in each face,
That faithful mirror wherein are expressed
The slumbering passions of the human breast.

Their rude and simple hut bespoke their sphere,
But love, content and happiness dwelt there;
The straw-thatched roof and sand-besprinkled floor,
An air of comfort spread around the poor.
The rustic porch o'er which the woodbine climbs,
The lattice windows of the olden times;
The neat trimmed garden fill'd with showy flowers
Economizes all his leisure hours:
The cottage beehive's in the garden found,
The bees with humming music hovering round.

Arcadian scenes present themselves to sight,
And to the rural fields and lanes invite,
Far from the public haunts and busy throng,
The woodlark cheers with its melodious song ;
The buzzing insect sailing through the air,
Weaves its soft music like a seraph there ;
The pearly dew descends upon the flowers,
Distill'd from heaven in softly falling showers ;
A snowy turban wraps their drooping heads,
Till morning wakes them from their drapery beds.
Rock'd in their cradles in the lofty trees,
The rooks are sung to slumber by the breeze ;
The grand old cedars stretch into the sky,
A thousand voices faintly murmur by ;
The foaming torrent leaps the rugged hill,
And in its channel turns the busy mill ;
Then winds capriciously in sylvan shades,
Struggling like one in fetters through the glades ;
Along its bank the pensive wanderer guides,
Through thirsty valleys where it gently glides.
Peculiar emblem of the life of man,
Who treads the stage without a settled plan,
Led by capricious fortune from his birth,
Through all the mazy windings of the earth.

Around, the circling hills retreating rise,
And the eye rivets on the crimson skies,
Where heaven and earth seem lock'd in fond embrace,
Each looking in the other's beaming face ;
The fertile meadows and the landscape round,
The balmy air and sweetly plaintive sound
From yonder copse, where from some hollow tree
The cuckoo fills the woods with minstrelsy.
The melancholy songstress pours from far
Her nightly vespers to the evening star ;
From pastoral slopes dull sounds the tinkling bell,
That guides the scatter'd flock by its dull knell ;
Where the green liveries grace this happy isle,
And nature wears one universal smile ;
Where flowers distil a perfume through the day,
And laden honey-bees in lindens play ;
When the earth's breast is swelling with delight,
Spreading a pleasing landscape to the sight ;
When rural melodies fall on the ear,
And golden harvests in their pride appear ;
When elevated objects all combine,
To fill the soul with ecstacy divine.

The cheering lamp of night looms in the west,
The peasantry retire to early rest,

Sweet Philomela pipes her plaintive lay,
And murmuring zephyrs through the lime trees play,
The studious owl sits moping on the tree,
And looks a judge in his wig dignity.
Through the wide vault a solemn stillness reigns,
The brawling brook runs through its winding veins,
O'er which the willows wave a plaintive sigh,
And aspens tremble as it murmurs by.

Far from the busy scenes of crowded life,
The seats of industry and haunts of strife,
Where, in perpetual motion like the tide,
The congregated mass spreads far and wide,
The village Church next our attention draws,
And brings the moraliser to a pause.
Near to the village green retired it stands,
And looks o'er all the farmer's smiling lands;
The ivy creeps around its turret tower,
Shielding from tempests when they gathering low'r;
The antiquated porch and pointed style,
And lancet windows of the sacred pile,
Bespeak its gothic character and age ;
A heavenly beacon in our pilgrimage.

The lofty tower points out the wanderer's way,
As homeward he returns at close of day.
Through sylvan vales the churchyard overlooks,
And rural lanes as serpentine as brooks,
With hedges lined on either side with thorns,
And groves of sheltering trees and mansion lawns.

Soul-soothing spot! where fancy loves to stray,
Aërial voices ominously play:
How oft when crimson clouds have streak'd the sky,
And festoon'd curtains of the east drew nigh,
When fluttering hope's illuminating beams
The recluse's mind fill'd with delusive dreams,
And o'er his spirit threw a joyous glow,
A sunset calmness and prospective shew;
When the world's promises of hope had fled,
And left their shadows in his aching head,
How oft in pensive sadness has he sought,
Your grave-stone chronicles in pious thought,
To calm th' o'erflowing surges of his breast,
And soothe his mind (deranged by thought) to rest.
To school his soul in its sepulchral gloom,
And dry those sorrows which the heart consume;

Though high the tide of feeling in him rose,
These tender grateful records would compose
Some private sorrow,—some domestic grief,
Which med'cine cannot cure or give relief;
Then through the mind's dark atmosphere would rise,
Like circling rainbows in the stormy skies,
Some glimmering rays his spirit to illume,
Some bright'ning prospect breaking through the gloom!

Yes, there are moments in our measured span
Of life when we throw off the stoic man:
Who has not, when his thoughts direct their flight
To distant regions in the depths of night,
The world forgetting, felt a purer flow
Of sense and feeling far surpassing show?
Who has not paused upon his worldly state,
And felt an interest in his future fate?
When earth's physicians who can do no more,
In dangerous cases give their patient o'er?
While weeping friends are gather'd round the room,
And threat'ning Death stands beckoning to the tomb:
Kind Heaven does thus its gentle dews impart,
And spreads its soft'ning influence through the heart;
To righteous meditation we incline,
And spiritually feel we're half divine.

This is the nursery of tender thought,
And here the breast with silent grief is fraught.
'Tis here the wrecks of human nature dwell,
And monuments their scanty history tell.
With slow and tottering step the aged poor,
On sabbath evenings stroll the churchyard o'er,
To look upon the grave of one they knew,
As if their piercing eyes would worm it through ;
Their dreaming minds in silence love to trace,
As in a glass, the late familiar face ;
Recall some action or some favourite phrase,
Some waggish jest or byword to his praise.
Yon lonely figure, in dark widow's weeds,
Behind those tombs from public gaze recedes,
To muse o'er him in life she held most dear,
And vent her sorrows in a pensive tear !

Ye silent speaking tablets of the dead,
Where at your feet lie in their narrow bed
The great, the small, the good, the bad, the proud,
Their ashes mingling in the silent crowd.
The hoary-headed sexton with his spade,
Remembers well each tenant and where laid,

A marble monument the rich supply,
The poor in osier graves neglected lie.
Rich sculptured figures stand in bold relief,
With angels bending o'er the tomb in grief ;
Their flattering inscriptions catch the eye,
Which interest the stranger passing by ;
Some dear memorial or holy text,
Divide our thoughts 'tween this world and the next !

Lo ! here is one to melt the hardest heart,
To blanche the cheek and bid the tear to start ;
The record tells her lineage, name, and youth,
So artlessly it bears the stamp of truth.
Oh ! gentle spirit, amiable, and mild,
With all th' endearing graces of a child,
And feminine attractions taking root
In one's affections ! now so cold, so mute !
Who is not pleased to see the rosebuds bloom ?
Who but must grieve when scatter'd to the tomb .
The lilies of the Spring, so pure, so sweet,
So pale, so delicate, lie at our feet
In beauty withering ! will they e'er revive,
Who were the most beloved on earth alive ?
Death no distinction knows ; the good and fair
Are his peculiar favourites, and lie there.

His march extends not o'er the barren plain,
But through the thick inhabited domain.
The Earth was much too small for such as thee,
Who soared above and grasp'd infinity.
Yet there are moments when we pensive grow,
Abstracted from the world and all below,
When we have lost a friend to memory dear,
And pine alone, and drop the tender tear !

A new raised stone, 'midst moss-grown others here.
Attention draws, and claims a passing tear ;
The grass-grown graves in little hillocks rise,
Studded with daisies opening to the skies,
But the loose earth smells fresh, no grass has grown.
Yet wither'd flowers all over it are strewn :
Some sweetly fresh which shed a perfume round,
Lie scatter'd on this new erected mound,
With wreaths immortal hung upon the cross,
To show some loving heart deplored her loss.
Oh ! I could kiss the gentle hand and bless
The heavenly soul that shewed such tenderness !

Close by in sympathy, a mournful yew
Hung gracefully its weeping head, and threw

A grateful shadow o'er the dear remains
Of one who felt the heart's acutest pains,
And never told her love, or breath'd his name,
But felt the smouldering passion kindle flame ;
And kept the lock'd-up secret of her breast,
And wasted slowly to her final rest.
Meek, patient, disappointed, and resign'd,
She lived on blighted hope and soon declined,
Closing her eyes, her last words were ' good night,'
And then to inner regions took her flight.

Here all our loved ones,—all our friendships part,
However dear and nearest to our heart.
That conqueror Death, who covets sire and son,
Has in all ages every battle won ;
The mightiest of all emperors, kings, and chiefs,
The wholesale ravisher of smiles and griefs,
Whose universal law and sceptre rules
Slaves, masters, statesmen, princes, lords, and fools.

Again the dirge of yonder muffled bell,
Booms forth its deep and melancholy knell ;
Another funeral cortège passes by,
The mourners stifled with a heartfelt sigh ;

The car with jet-black horses creeps along,
Attended by the mute respectful throng,
Towards the yawning grave, when standing round,
Again is heard that mournful tolling sound,
Like a sepulchral voice, as if it said,
' I am the spirit of the sleeping dead !'
Around the grave in sable costume stood
The weeping relatives in gown and hood,
While ' dust to dust' was echoed from the tomb,
Which o'er them cast a solemn death-like gloom.

This was the funeral of the village belle,
Whose winning manners threw a magic spell,
Whose beauty took you captive at first sight,
Like an enchantress, and bewitched you quite ;
Whose glittering spirits, like reviving Spring,
A joyous sunshine all around you fling,
Warming the genial current of your vein,
And quick'ning the slow motion of the brain ;
A period when the tendrils of the vine,
Cling for support, and fondly intertwine.
So the affections twine around the heart,
And instincts of our nature love impart.

To a fine figure and a Grecian face,
Were added simple elegance and grace,
Without the vanity they oft inspire,
For heaven had destined her for regions higher.
Benevolence and sympathy of mind
Enlarged her generous heart for all mankind ;
She sought to heal the miseries they endure,
In daily visits to the friendless poor,
The sick, the blind, the orphan, and the school ;
She read them lessons and she taught by rule ;
O'er mental darkness shedding sparks of light,
And solacing the soul with spiritual sight.

No marvel she should admiration raise,
And grateful hearts and tongues be fill'd with praise ;
She was all goodness, purity, and love,
Celestial influence aiding from above.
This charming girl was taken by surprise,
By one who could not all he felt disguise ;
Her youth and lively spirits prepossess'd,
Consuming fire was smouldering in his breast,
And to the tender passion he confess'd !

No stranger he, for at the Doctor's ball,
Amongst the guests, athletic, handsome, tall,

Of military air, this son of Mars
Blazed like a meteor amongst the stars.
His fond attachment sparkled in his eyes,
He felt the transport of his soul to rise ;
As to an angel he did homage pay,
And nought could chase her from his thoughts away :
Her presence like an inspiration given,
A seraph seem'd who points the way to heaven ;
Her absence like a meteor pass'd from sight,
Was like the dreary desert without light.

He wooed and won ; the nuptial day was fix'd,
Each for the other only did exist ;
To him she yielded her ingrafted heart,
And each became the other's counterpart ;
The day arrived when she became his wife,
And partner in earth's fortunes for her life :
They made the usual monthly wedding tour,
Where nature's grandest, loftiest scenes allure,
Mix'd with the picturesque which all surround,
Where something new in every step is found,
While admiration lingers to survey
The charming prospects of a cloudless day,

Feeling a mutual pleasure at the sight,
And a new thrilling transport of delight,
In their seclusion from the public gaze,
When heavenly bliss emits its genial rays,
When blushing modesty in concert shewn,
Courting retirement, wished to be alone.

Three happy weeks were pass'd in leisure there,
Free from anxiety and worldly care,
When unexpectedly to their surprise,
A telegram dispatch 'official' flies,
With special orders summoning him hence,
To join his regiment, and his march commence
For foreign service! war had been declared;
The Russian eagle England's lion dared!

This news was stunning, and the colour flew
From both their cheeks, and left a livid hue;
The shock was like an earthquake, so acute,
It paralysed them, and they both stood mute:
He first broke silence as he look'd aghast,
To see her count'nance changed and overcast
With melancholy; for her dream of joy,
Nipp'd in the blossom all her hopes destroy,

And statue-like remain'd unmoved and fix'd,

As in a trance, and seem'd not to exist !

His quivering words fell on her listless ear,

In choking accents and a voice not clear,

To th' intent it was his country's call,

And by his honour he must stand or fall.

Ambition ! glory ! military fame !

Would wreathe a crown of glory round his name ;

Promotion, fortune, laurels him await,

And she would share those honours soon or late.

She grew resign'd, it was the will of Fate !

The rail and steam soon sever'd him from shore,

He waved adieu till he could see no more.

All seem'd to her an evanescent dream,

A vivid flash of lightning's piercing gleam ;

Life was a wilderness now he was gone,

And in society she felt alone.

She watch'd the ship news,—dreamt of him at night,

Thought on his promise frequently to write,—

Look'd on his photograph,—her wedding ring,

And locket, souvenirs, and everything

As pledges of affection he had given ;

And for his welfare supplicated heaven.

At last the wished-for letter was received
From Scutari's camp, and her mind relieved.
It breathed affection, shadow'd forth the hour
Of happy meeting in their nuptial bower.
The next epistle came from Alma's height,
After the battle, and described the fight.
Night fires turn pale before approaching morn,
And beat of drum alarms at early dawn ;
Three hours terrific slaughter madly raged,
While gun to gun, and man to man engaged ;
When glorious vict'ry follow'd the allies,
Before whose prowess the wild Cossack flies.
The next post was from Balaklava town,
Conspicuous for misfortune as renown
And terrible disaster ! Cathcart hill,
Bewails with monuments its heroes still.
A gallant band of horsemen cross the plain
To charge an army ! and were quickly slain ;
Chivalrous courage marked the enterprise,
The whole field view'd the useless sacrifice !
One letter illustrated Inkerman,
How in the depth of night th' attack began,
When suddenly the desperate Russ appear'd
In a dense fog their enemies to beard ;

And in their tents the English force surprised,
Who with th' allies the enemy chastised.
Then came the siege of wall'd Sebastopol,
And the stern winter of the frozen pole,
With all the horrors of a savage war,
Want, cold, and misery, and the scenes they saw.
The tedious trenching, round which earthworks run,
The dreary watch, and constant booming gun,
The night surprises of the treacherous foe,
The toil and hardships forced to undergo ;
With wearisome anxiety of mind,
And failing health, with other woes they find,
Brought many a victim to an early grave,
Whose tactics and whose courage could not save,
And with them Blanche's brave and honour'd lord,
A gallant officer beloved, adored !

In mourning costume and in widow's weeds,
She in retirement on her sorrow feeds,
The crimson rose that wither'd on her face,
Had left a pale white lily in its place.
A parasite had crept into her heart,
And spread its venom through to every part.

The loss of spirits and her prostrate state,
Were signs and symbols of approaching fate ;
Her heart was broken ! all she loved was gone !
And like a sea-girt rock she stood alone ;
Then wasted to a shadow day by day,
Resign'd to Fate's decree, and pass'd away !

Oft the reflective mirror of our mind
Revives the past of youth we left behind,
And opens up rich veins of solid gold
Before our future dawn'd, when we grow old !
One reminiscence, giving new delight,
Looms in the distance and breaks forth to sight ;
'Tis sabbath morning, cheerful and serene,
And there again around the village green
Appears the Sunday school in best attire,
A scene which even sceptics might admire,
Wending their way to church amid the throng,
The tolling church-bell tripping them along.
What day-dream happiness does life appear,
Thus illustrated through the rolling year !
Care has not writ its lines upon their brow,
Nor robb'd the spirits of their genial glow.

All work suspended on this day of rest,
Both sexes flock to church in all their best,
To hear the gospel and to join in prayer,
To sing His praises, and for Heaven prepare,
Their souls communing with the Lord on high,
Their buoyant hopes fix'd on Eternity :
From earthly thoughts and worldly cares shut out,
All tranquil-minded, serious, and devout.
A day of worship and of calm repose,
Free from anxieties and worldly woes.
The swelling organ falls upon the ear,
In solemn soothing whispers, soft and clear,
When the Squire's family appears in view,
Conducted by the verger to their pew ;
A retinue of servants sit behind,
And silence with solemnity is join'd.
The sacred service then at once begun,
And all their singing hearts were joined in one ;
The liturgy responded by the whole,
Was meat and drink to the believing soul.
The written sermon, orthodox and trite,
Was to their intellect a lamp of light,
Which shewed them how to live in bonds of love,
And how to worship the great Judge above :

Which riveted attention to the last,
And over all a holy influence cast,
Connecting the great future and the past.
The discourse ended, no one left his seat,
Until the worthy baronet's retreat,
When the assembly rose with one accord,
And follow'd out the fendatory lord,
Who, true to custom, with his daughters walk'd,
And with them o'er the written discourse talk'd.
The crowd respectfully in groups behind,
Join'd in their track, till all their dwelling find.
The entrance lodge was guarded by a gate,
Kept by a pensioner upon th' estate,
Infirm and drooping like the setting sun,
After the race of life is nearly run.
The long and sweeping walk ran, opening wide,
Between the shrubbery on either side,
With specimens of pine and cedars rare,
And auracaria from the Himalaya,
And here and there an avenue of trees,
Shelter'd from scorching sun or cutting breeze,
Which in the face of day grew dim and dark,
And led up to the mansion in the park,
Whose broad walk terraces and open views,
From rustic seats delight you and amuse.

To look back on our youth, and it recall,
Seems like a vision and a festival,
With mingled feelings we the past review,
When all was bright and life itself was new,
When innocence skipt lightly on the wing,
And spinning-top was dozing in the ring,
Or gaudy kite was wing'd into the air,
'Midst tiers of clouds and kept a pris'ner there ;
Or airy bubbles blown off from the bowl.
Emblems of life and laughter of the soul ;
The martial drill, the art of self defence,
Gymnastic feats, or speech of eloquence ;
The graceful dance with music to inspire,
Reciting parts of dramas all admire ;
The rival race or cricket-match, and games
So new and various, legion are their names !
Thus step by step we up to manhood climb,
And then perceive the sands of fleeting time ;
But, as we ripen, cares of life invade,
And man must some profession learn, or trade,
His paradise of happiness to lose,
With the seraphic visions of the Muse.

Oft will my youth in fond remembrance rise,
When childhood's fleeting joys crowd on my eyes ;

Oft swells my heart in sympathy for those,
Who now enjoy the Eden-like repose,
From golden dream they're destined soon to wake,
To meet with conflicts which may crush and break :
Oft would reflection mirror in my mind,
And fond remembrance all my youth unbind,
When o'er me open'd an unclouded sky,
And temporary ills pass'd swiftly by ;
When, every care forgotten with the day,
'Twas like a long and sunshine holiday !
The sunbeams smile upon our happiest hours,
But far too soon the hovering tempest lours,
Leaving the fairy images imprest
In fancy pictures and the heaving breast :
Mere phantoms that have lived and pass'd away,
Like virgin beauty into dust or clay.

Yon winding river musically sweet,
Sings as it courses to its copse retreat,
Presenting on its banks of velvet green,
The rural meadow and the pastoral scene ;
The gentle shepherd with his buxom maid,
Seek some tall oak or chesnut's friendly shade,

Mixing their sweet discourse with pipe and song.

To cheer the purling stream of time along.

Meandering minstrel of the rolling year,

Weaving delicious music to the ear.

As if in fond remembrance of the Bard,

Whose intellectual genius we regard

With gazing admiration, and stand by

His marble bust in mute idolatry !

On Avon's banks his spirit oft is heard,

And haunts you like the singing of a bird,

Then flitting past floats down the hallow'd stream,

Like the dim shadow of a fading dream ;

And doubles through the rich and park-like grounds,

Encircling yon stone mansion which it bounds,

Where dwells the honoured, loved, and worthy Squire.

The sovereign of the soil, whom all admire ;

Renown'd for hospitality and race,

With great good nature in his happy face,

Radiant with health and kindliness of heart,

Which did a cheerfulness to all impart :

Gracious in manner, affable, polite,

He gained esteem and confidence at sight.

His genial nature made you feel at ease,

His wish and disposition were to please.

As Justice of the Peace, his look was grave,
And duty triumphed o'er his will to save.
A word in season, with his kind advice,
Oft had its influence and wean'd from vice.
A relic of the light of other days,
He was antique in dress and all his ways;
A patriarch in age, who lived by rule,
A model of the old ancestral school.
Descended from a long paternal line,
Amongst th' illustrious he was born to shine;
A county member,—one of the élite,
Possessing large domains and country seat;
His politics were of the tory breed,
Who cling to 'good old times' as to their creed,
A stationary class, who fail to see
The change and progress of society:
Who think the world for them alone was made,
And not for mushroom millionaires of trade.
True to the principles within him bred,
He loved all country sports and took the lead;
Walking and riding were his daily fare,
Hunting and shooting his peculiar care;
Early his habits, regular and plain,
Sir William was a gentlemanly thane;

A social neighbour no one would offend,

A liberal master and the poor man's friend.

The good old servants in his service died,

His tenants felt a pleasure and a pride

To take his counsel ; twice a year the Hall

Re-echoed with the merry festival :

When rent-day came it was a holiday,

And ten per cent. off made them all look gay ;

When youth and age rejoiced o'er dainty food,

And revelled with delight in good home-brew'd :

Cracked nuts and jokes with shouts of laughter long.

Join'd in the dance or chorus of the song ;

Life's cares were banish'd, all was fun and mirth,

For all combin'd to make a heaven of earth.

The charming pleasure-grounds were open thrown,

And in their gay attire both sexes shone.

In clustering groups they roved th' Elysian fields,

And the air echoed with their joyous peals ;

The timorous fawn was startled from its lair,

By the hired band whose music fill'd the air.

The dear old Squire and family appear'd

Upon the lawn, and all their faces cheer'd

With social intercourse and heart-felt glee :

In truth it was a Paradise to see !

Among the visitors upon the ground,
Or at the feast, the minister was found,
The twin companion and the bosom friend
Of him who could so much enjoyment lend
To life's dull routine, scattering bliss around,
A true philanthropist and heavenward bound.
They had been chums at the collegiate school,
Their friendship ripen'd and had ne'er grown cool :
And when the late respected Vicar died,
The benefice was given to Reverend Hyde.
There is no sphere of life we could embrace
More beneficial to the human race,
When the blest hands of charity impart
The finest touches of the human heart,
Or when the soul, to meditation given,
Divides our thoughts between this world and heaven ;
Seeking the consolation of that light,
Divine and spiritual beyond our sight ;
Then comes the saint-like messenger to guide,
Who stands a guardian angel at our side.

The living was three hundred pounds a year,
His worth unknown by all who held him dear :

He walk'd with God and took an active part,
In culturing mind and in enlarging heart ;
Did good by stealth, and visited the poor,
Called on the sick and took receipts to cure ;
Discoursed and comforted both youth and age,
With texts of scripture from the sacred page.
And, like his model, influenced for good,
Perform'd his mission with solicitude.
In petty disputes (men will disagree)
They nominated him their referee ;
He was their counsel, jury, judge, and friend,
On whose impartial judgment they depend :
He practised what he preach'd,—spoke without fear,
And to his calling, faithful and sincere,
The spiritual physician of the soul,
Who train'd and raised it for its final goal.

Few are the leading characters of note,
Within my album sketches I can quote,
In which the world would any interest find,
Or care to have engraved upon the mind ;
Yet there are portraits in the living crowd,
Of either sex we might be justly proud,

And single out for popular applause,

Active and useful agents in the cause

Of social duty, binding man to man,

In one communion, and harmonious plan!

The Doctor largely draws on our esteem,

A benefactor to his kind we deem,

Not the mean sordid wretch who lives for self

And follows his profession for mere pelf;

A nobler spirit in his nature dwells,

Than in the mercenary who buys and sells.

His art's to cure disease and life prolong,

To soothe afflictions which to man belong,

To trace his sufferings and find out their cause,

And remedy complaints by natural laws,

To amputate the limb and heal the wound,

For antidotes to search the wide world round,

A damaged constitution to restore,

And health where sickness domiciled before.

In foreign countries where his art's unknown,

What confidence and gratitude are shewn!

His cures are miracles,—his drugs are balm,

That work a potent sybilean charm,

O'er all their senses, lulling them to rest,

Oh! 'tis worth living for to be thus bless'd

For surgery he had a special call,
But general practice served the turns of all ;
The very Hippocrates of the place,
He was consulted with in every case ;
And rivals in the villages around
Came for advice and found his dogmas sound.
When out of health we patiently endure
The nauseous med'cine till we find a cure.
Into his keeping we ourselves resign,
In general sickness and in deep decline.
This confidential intercourse imparts
Mutual esteem and friendship in our hearts.
In dangerous cases, when kind friends despair,
How watchful his attention and his care !
His skill is to the utmost taxed ; you trace
The hopes and fears depicted in his face ;
His visits are more frequent night and day,
His anxious mind induces him to stay
Until the looked for change !—the crisis o'er,
We feel a kinder friendship than before ;
Our gratitude o'erflows,—our flood of grief,
Now that the dear one's saved, has found relief.
His portly frame, good humour, kind address,
Engaging manners, natural cheerfulness,

The spirits of his patients would revive,
Season'd with anecdote that made alive,
And o'er their feelings threw a joyous glow,
Which made them half forget their present woe;
So useful he in various kinds of ways
Deserves our notice and commands our praise.

Next in importance, character, degree,
The Village Lawyer claims priority;
So various are the ills of human life,
So prone to evil, and so given to strife,
That life and property, by all held dear,
Would not be sacred but for law, 'tis clear!
All need assistance to redress their wrong,
Sex against sex,—the weak against the strong!
Our statutes framed alike for rich and poor,
The halls of Justice open wide their door
For daily suitors; through the law's delay
(Glorious uncertainty in every way),
Expense, anxiety, and restless nights,
Threat'ning to ruin, keep us from our rights;
And many born to title and estate,
Read in their lives the harsh decrees of fate.

Theft, trespass, insult, meet with prompt redress,
With paltry crimes which criminals confess.
Th' attorney is engaged on either side,
And right or wrong the magistrates decide ;
He's by his clients paid to do his best,
To accuse or to defend the guiltiest.
One branch of his profession 's to convey,
By deeds, all kinds of property away,
And settlements upon our wedding day ;
Another to make wills ere we retire
In the calm evening sunset to expire !

In yon retreating house with gable wing,
The noisy sounds of babbling voices ring,
For there assembled is the Village school,
The seat of learning, discipline, and rule.
The raw material here instruction gain,
And useful knowledge 's stored into the brain,
For after-use in the wide world's domain !
That much depends upon ourselves we preach,
But how much more on pedagogues who teach ?
All honour to th' instructors of our youth,
Who culture mind, and lead the way to truth !

A blessing on the man who does impart
Light to the soul and virtue to the heart!
Right principles instill'd when we are young,
Like early lessons in our mother tongue,
Leave their impressions on the budding mind,
Long after our tuition 's left behind,
Grateful remembrance makes us passing kind
To those who trained us and won our esteem,
When entrance into life looks like a dream!
Such was the feeling entertain'd for one,
Who scatter'd darkness 'fore the rising sun,
And cleared the hazy atmosphere about,
Before the sparks of intellect burst out.
Firm, resolute, impartial, his command
Was law! and broken brought his reprimand:
Order, arrangement, method, form, and rule,
Were the marked features of the Village school;
Ill tempers, vicious habits, dogged will,
Require the master's management, and skill.
The innate disposition of the child,
Like a young foal unbroken, will run wild.
'Tis our instructor's business and aim,
To discipline, to conquer, mould, and tame.
In every feature lines of care you trace,
With Greek and Latin in his wither'd face.

His widespread fame and praises loud were sung,
For classic literature and foreign tongue.
In early youth he served as tutor here,
And training boys seem'd his peculiar sphere ;
Though dry and dull, monotonous and slow,
The art of teaching does on masters grow,
And beams of pleasure light the studious eye,
To see the youngsters pass their seniors by
In upper classes, and to merit rise,
And carry off the honours and first prize.

In towns the Market-place, Exchange, Town-hall,
Assembly rooms, museums, attract us all,
And give an interest which the village lacks,
Where all around are farms and barns and stacks,
With browsing sheep and cattle scatter'd wide,
And farmyard poultry feeding side by side
In peace and plenty : smiling sheaves of grain,
Are ripening in the sunshine swell'd with rain,
Giving a promise of a bounteous yield,
From every waving—every golden field.
In hay or harvest time at early dawn,
The reapers mow the grass and bearded corn,

And helping wives and children strew the fields,
To gather in the crop that plenty yields;
Filling with joy the farmer's grateful heart,
Dependent upon weather as on art.
His life is spent in quietude and ease,
A passive state which gentle spirits please,
Much envied and to which we all aspire,
When from life's storms and conflicts we retire;
A peaceful haven and a calm retreat,
With smiles of love and plenty at our feet;
Hayricks surround his homestead neatly thatch'd,
With wheat and barley waiting to be thrash'd;
And milch cows, turkeys, geese, and pigs besides,
O'er which the farmyard sentinel presides,
Whose growling throat its deaf'ning thunder pours,
In angry volumes and resounding roars;
Train'd carrier pigeons round their dove-cot fly,
And circling skim the ocean and the sky.
The neighbouring peasantry turn out to glean
In family groups, as in the distance seen,
Whose frugal savings sent to yonder mill,
Now waves its wind-sails on the foremost hill.
The busy windmill slowly grinds the corn,
And o'er the hills is heard the huntsman's horn,

With all th' attractions of the starting place,
And all th' excitement of the lively chase.

Oh ! what a cheerful, joyous sight to see,
All join'd in love the human family !
Th' invited guest-haymakers of the mead,
Who in the general frolic take the lead :
Both sexes join the fun, and help to make
The rising corn-stacks with pitchfork and rake.
Most come to feast upon the carrying day,
And not to work, but dance, joke, sing, and play :
The new-mown fields with peals of laughter rung,
And jollity inspired the mirthful young ;
The gentler sex look on with bashful glance,
But show their preference for the country dance :
Their counterpart, by nature rude and rough,
Leap, box, and wrestle or play blindman's buff :
A pic-nic party making holiday,
Was never more disposed for joy and play,
Or for the plentiful substantial fare,
Which agricultural gatherings duly share.

Few entertainments giv'n beyond a ball,
Except the feast or Christmas festival,

When hospitality is at its height,
And all for miles around their friends invite,
To the best cheer their open homes impart,
When they give freely and with all their heart ;—
Make village life a flat and dull affair,
Without the private dance or public fair ;
A christening or a wedding may amuse,
And country sports an interest infuse,
In the game season, or exciting chase,
With fishing, football, cricket-match, or race.
But the attractive little Village Inn,
Has all the comforts of a home within,
Where genial spirits in the evening meet,
In social intercourse and snug retreat,
To enjoy the exhilarating cup of cheer,
The soothing pipe or billiard-table here,
With news, discourse, and politics to hear :
Though much condemn'd by the domestic wife,
'Tis an oasis in the country life.
Here private clubs and public meetings drew
The village chiefs and humbler classes too,
In that long large assembly room of state,
Where lectures, concerts, dinners, and debate,
Give local interest to the sluggish place,
Which seldom wears a smile upon its face.

Besides the magnates who were born and bred,
And in all public matters took the lead.
Stars of less magnitude located near,
Who shed a lustre round their private sphere ;
Relieved from business or official place,
After the battle of life's busy chase.
Dearer to him than all the spots of Earth,
Man has a yearning for his place of birth,
Attracted to a distant foreign shore,
He fondly hopes to visit it once more ;
If not to settle down in life's decline,
Upon the old estate beneath his vine ;
Recalling the hilarity and joy,
Felt when an unsophisticated boy,
Whence simple innocence creates a flush
Of mingled feelings in the crimson blush,
When home's sweet comforts,—smiles of soft'ning love,
Impart resemblance to the blest above.
Who has not felt his heart within him beat,
When home returning to his country seat ?
Who has not shrunk when bidding those farewell,
Perhaps for ever, whom he loves so well ?

As through a picture gallery we stray,
And find ourselves attracted on the way,

By *this* amusing work,—*that* gem of art,
Which fascinate the eye or touch the heart;
So we must linger on our Village tour,
To sketch some portraits of the upper floor;
Assembled round the winter-evening fire,
In the enjoyment of all they desire.
In the respectable and homely Inn,
Stored with malt liquor, brandy, rum, and gin;
Some come to be amused, to see and hear,
While sipping down their tumbler of good cheer;
Some come to speak and take an active part,
In the discussion the day's news impart.

The little parlour round which drawings hung,
With bacchanalian encores often rung,
And cheered with vocal harmony the soul,
Through which a rapturous enchantment stole,
Which sweeten'd labour, calmed the knitted brow,
And o'er each count'nance threw a genial glow.
Snug quarters these for travellers from afar,
Or native guests who used the landlord's bar,
Whose pretty daughter, with her gracious smile,
Affable manners and coquettish style,

Was the alluring magnet of the Inn,
Which with good liquors drew the public in.

Here an old Captain, who had ploughed the seas,
Dropt anchor and retired to take his ease,
In the ancestral Hall where he was born,
Behind the avenue and spacious lawn,
Adorn'd with variegated shrubs and flowers,
With a few forest trees and rustic bowers :
Red-brick'd and of the Elizabethan style,
A plain, substantial, venerable pile,
That spoke of good old times and memories dear,
Which oft in spectral shadows reappear.
His figure was robust, and short and stout,
Though cross'd with care and subject to the gout :
His weather-beaten face and fading eye
Shew'd the right side of sixty had passed by ;
Although his hazy countenance would rise
Like morning sunbeams of the gilded skies,
When he grew warm and felt an inward glow
Of feeling and excitement overflow,
While he depicted an adventure bold,
Hairbreadth escapes and narratives well told,

Incidents of the voyages he made,
In distant climes for purposes of trade.
Such a companion one is pleased to meet.
Though bluff in manner, rough, and indiscreet
In language, which the seaman unrefined
And blunt, lets loose when speaking out his mind :
There's such an honest openness of heart
Stamp'd in his nature, we reluctant part.

Amongst the visitors who came to spend
A leisure hour and gossip with a friend,
Or read the news, or spout, or criticise,
Of fresh complexion, and of middle size,
Lively in manner, and of sunset date,
Clear in conception, and fond of debate,
A gentleman reduced, of manners mild,
While differing in opinion often smiled
At narrow minds with a sarcastic sneer,
When proving what to his own mind was clear ;
With logic, figures, theories, and views,
Which sound or unsound failed not to amuse,
A widower he with two fair daughters blest,
Consumption's blight had nipp'd off all the rest.

In a small village everybody's known,
Each makes the other's business his own ;
Gossip and scandal like contagion spread,
And all are publish'd, criticised and read,
Libell'd, dissected, and to pieces torn,
From cradle innocence when newly born.

There was a visitor attired in black,
Open to calumny and rude attack,
Who settled in the outskirts of the town,
A living mystery, and little known,
Cold, taciturn, methodical, and grave,
Liberal in politics, no party's slave ;
Firm, modest, independent, and well read,
He listen'd in debate to what was said,
But seldom spoke, from diffidence and fear,
For he was not collected, prompt, or clear :
Reserved, unequal, dull, and sometimes stern,
You could not all his character discern ;
Cheerful to-day, gay, eloquent, and bright,
To-morrow dismal as an anchorite ;
His code of morals, too, was so severe,
The volatile thought he was most austere :

Abstracted in a reverie or dream,
And all absorb'd, he deaf and dumb would seem :
For his imagination took delight,
In the transparent scenes of mental sight,
The future rather than the present state,
And metaphysical ideas of fate.
The germs of poesy flow'd from his tongue,
Whence eloquence and flow'rs of fancy sprung.
This silent, sentimental cast of mind,
Made him appear a stranger 'mongst mankind,
And not the social being God design'd.
He look'd an alien in his native land,
And e'en himself he failed to understand ;
Lost in bewilderment of thought he walks
Alone, and absent, and unconscious talks :
A thorough sceptic to the general creed,
He ventilated all that he believed.
A votary of the muse, he loved to quote
The ancient bards, and bards of modern note,
In illustration of his private view,
And his whole soul in glowing fancy threw,
Wandering in realms of fiction by the light
Of the mind's mirror and ideal sight.
He had been crossed in love when in his prime,
Which half deranged him, and he scribbled rhyme :

This tinged his mind with sadness and despair,

Which gave his face a gloomy thoughtful air,

And wrecked his hopes of happiness awhile,

For he could seldom counterfeit a smile.

The world to him was sunless and a shade,

Beneath whose withering look all blessings fade :

Earth was a desert, life a solitude,

And friends who called found him in cheerless mood.

Commercial business occupied his life,

And rhymes his leisure in the place of wife ;

His leaning posture and projecting head,

Shew'd to the office desk he had been bred.

'Twas thus the sentimental habit grew,

And o'er him cast its pale and sickly hue ;

Industrious, persevering, and self raised,

The exalted great and eminent he praised ;

Impulsive, cautious, and by nature proud,

He kept aloof and shunn'd the vulgar crowd ;

Those padlock'd lips his secrets kept conceal'd,

As if they were hermetically seal'd.

Time hasten'd on, the vision pass'd away,

And through his count'nance beamed returning day,

As after an eclipse resembling night
The shadow passes and restores the light;
So out of chaos order was restored,
Another Venus rose to be adored.
The anchorite wall'd up within himself,
Dead to the world, and laid upon the shelf,
From his own ashes, Phœnix-like revived,
And felt the like delirium still survived,
The warmer passions kindle into flame,
And the pulse quickens through his nervous frame.
Love follow'd admiration, hermit life
Was changed for the companionship of wife,
Whose genial qualities and generous heart
A ray of cheerfulness to all impart,
Charming the circle with her spirits bright,
And gladd'ning all who came within her sight;
Whose magic wand gave comfort to the poor,
And scatter'd bliss at every cottage door;
Whose acute sympathies for all mankind
Shone in her actions, and her feeling mind.
In secret she delighted to do good,
And felt an interest and solicitude
In the soul's welfare, while she loved to teach
The ignorant-minded, and her maxims preach:

Warm-hearted, natural, affable, sincere,
Attracting all who came within her sphere,
Affectionate and kind, a faithful friend,
On whose firm principles you might depend,
She lived beloved, and her sweet influence spread,
As if by some superior being led !

There are some vestiges amongst us cast,
Belonging to the venerable past,
Of men who have outlived their friends and time ;
Ghosts of a bygone age when in their prime,
Who prate of good old customs,—golden days,
In all the glowing imagery of praise,
Exalting everything beyond compare,
From the crusaders down to Christmas fare,
Repeating o'er and o'er the prosy tale,
Homespun, familiar, fabulous or stale.
Diluvian antiquaries !—men of dust !
Who smell of mouldy relics, coins, and rust.

Such was the student whom we now pourtray,
A living relic of a former day,
Who went about in his ancestral guise,
Open to critics and to sneering eyes,

In a quaint fashion,—doublet, coat, and hose,
Silk stockings, white cravat, and buckled shoes,
With powdered hair, frill'd shirt, and bouquet sweet,
And smart kid gloves, a gentleman complete.
A rare old specimen of England's pride,
To whom our modern fop is close allied,
A hypochondriac little understood,
A bookworm and of sentimental mood,
The winter settled on his frosty head,
And wreaths of silver locks around it spread;
His eye had lost its lustre and grown dim,
The staff supported now his tottering limb,
And nature shewed its universal sign
Of evening sunset and of life's decline.
The pilgrim moralist would lingering pause,
And fortify himself with Nature's laws;
For he had been accustomed to draw near,
To temple ruins, and to spots held dear
In history's records, their decline to trace,
And with devotion their remains embrace,
As sacred memorials of the past,
Of grey and crumbling edifices vast.
Learned in history he ransack'd the stores,
And entered the museums and library doors

To catch a glimpse of relics and pore o'er
The sites of famous nations now no more ;
Collecting fragments of antiquity,
Coins, fossils, gems, and books of rarity :
With sculpture's rich remains preserved in part,
And curiosities, and works of art ;
All coated over with time honour'd dust,
And eaten into by consuming rust.
He loved to muse in churchyards, and to read
The epitaphs in memory of the dead ;
To linger in the old ancestral halls,
The barrow ruins, and old turret walls ;
The hallow'd spots of earth, and abbey grounds,
Whose solemn echoes came like haunted sounds,
As if their former tenants watching near,
Would at their desecration reappear,
In spectral guise and supernatural wail,
(Before whose frown the stoutest heart might quail)
To hold from sacrilege all impious hands,
Threat'ning to blight and wither up their lands.

From his youth upward he had learn'd to pay
The homage due to age and to decay,

And in his continental tour when young,
Indulged his antiquarian taste among
Druidical remains, and Roman camps,—
Monastic ruins, and the cavern's damps,—
The christian church, the castle, donjon keep,—
And cemeteries where all so soundly sleep,
With all belonging to the days of yore,
Half buried in the dust and ivy'd o'er.

Near to our village, visited by few,
The spire of Stratford opens to our view,
From many points around the sylvan scene,
Th' attractive church is in the distance seen ;
The glassy Avon in its still retreat,
Through mazy windings warbles at its feet ;
The lofty towers of Warwick burst in sight,
With turret castle, elegant and light ;
And in the distance Kenilworth 's descried,
A skeleton of strength in fallen pride !
Recalling chivalry and tournament,
When gallant knights and squires in armour went ;
And myriads of archers throng'd the field,
Where cavaliers went forth with lance and shield.

To Charlecote or to Fulbrooke trace the stream,

And through their avenues of Shakespeare dream,

Whose haunting spirit seems to linger near ;

Sweet music whispering in the tuneful ear.

He fills you with the human and divine,

And like a seraph on you seems to shine ;

Imagination warming with a ray

Of inspiration conjures up a play :

In bas-relief both sexes seem to rise

In costumed characters before your eyes :

As represented on the public stage,

Exhibiting the manners of the age.

With storied incidents the drama teems,

The living world a great theatre seems,

Peopled with actors each in his own sphere,

In shifting scenes where all in turn appear ;

The human type of every land and race

Is brought before the audience face to face,

From every quarter and from every shore,

Of modern times as well as days of yore.

Faithful to nature, copyist of art,

He draws a fac simile of every part,

His comic scenes an interest infuse,

While his great aim is simply to amuse

And point a moral; searching round the earth
For representatives to give us mirth;
Holding the mirror up to nature's glass,
Reflecting specimens of every class,
Who satirise the customs of mankind,
Their vanities and selfishness of mind,
With pride, deception, scandal of the race,
Which pointedly is thrown into your face,
Where humorous dialogue sustains a part,
Or deep sincere affection tries the heart.
His tragic muse is naturally grave,
For death is solemn even to the brave;
The works of darkness are conceived in sin,
Revenge is plann'd the very heart within;
Excited passion boiling into rage
Is well pourtray'd upon the public stage;
The jealous element is hard to tame,
Impelled to action, murder is its aim;
Ambition prompts,—satanic influence leads,
E'en to the gates of hell by bloody deeds.
His lively fancy fairy forms creates,
And in romantic regions speculates,
Summoning spirits from the vasty deep,
And dream-like phantoms which appear in sleep;

With mythologic figures of the wood,
Aërial sylphs and sprites of solitude.

The ' Prince of Poets !' all the bards exclaim,
While all the world re-echoes with his fame :
His works are his best monuments and praise,
Although ' In Memory' we his altars raise ;
Wealth, rank, and fortune sink into the shade,
Compared with genius which can never fade :
And regal splendours—courts of beauty die,
But his is glorious immortality !
Strangers from far seek out his place of birth,
From every region of the sea-girt earth,
And pilgrims visit his sepulchral tomb,
Within the chancel's solitary gloom,
To gaze upon his mural bust, and stones
That hide his dust and venerable bones.

If round the world in restlessness we roam,
The heart's soft tendrils still will cling to home,
For ties of kindred, and domestic love,
Will melt the feelings, and affections move.
Oft will our memory's lamp when far away,
In the calm twilight of expiring day,

Light up those scenes familiar to our view,
With that dear dwelling where our boyhood grew,
And the sweet garden with its velvet lawn,
Which hybrid specimens and shrubs adorn ;
With mounds and banks, and sweet parterre of flowers,
And fragrant creepers round the rustic bowers,
All redolent with bloom and gay attire,
Whose charming freshness we so much admire ;
Whose beauteous colouring delights the eye,
And fills the fancy with its imagery.
Through shrubbery walks we wander unconfined,
At least in pictured prospects of the mind,
And conjure up the quiet pastoral scene,
Beyond in meadows of an emerald green ;
Fringed with the hawthorn hedge and belt of tre
To screen an eyesore, or divert the breeze,
Where joyous birds their various anthems raise,
In one grand concert to their Maker's praise !

Hail, lovely Village ! we return again,
From classic spots of interest which detain,
To thy attractions ! in the distance seen,
A group of nymphs are dancing on the green,

In merry laughter, and with sylph-like grace,
And happiness depicted in each face !
A rural custom filling with delight :
A little further, crowding on the sight,
Some ardent cricketers of robust frame,
All emulous pursue the manly game,
With earnest aim and ever anxious throw,
Or in the vigorous loud resounding blow.
There, yonder schoolboys just turn'd out for drill,
Marching like soldiers to display their skill.
Buoy'd up with courage, some for quarrels slight
Gird up their loins for pugilistic fight :
Or in gymnastic feats their muscles brace,
Or swift as wind run in th' exciting race ;
While some essay to leap, to fence or run,
And wrestle for amusement or for fun.

Like a child's placid face, the opening dawn
Gave promise of a bright and happy morn ;
The blood-red sun dispels the mist which hung,
The starlings and the finches welcome sung.
Awakening from their sleep the languid flowers,
Whose dews dissolving fall in silver showers,

Diffusing warmth and cheerfulness around,
And opening vistas which the distance bound.
The music of those laughter ringing bells,
The playful breeze with deep base echoes swells,
And every one looks pleased, spruce, dress'd, and gay,
For, joy of joys, this is the wedding day,
Of the young, blooming, beautiful Maria,
The eldest daughter of the portly Squire !
She was his comforter and darling child,
Sweet, modest, gentle, affable, and mild ;—
The evening star that watch'd his sun's decline,
A beau-ideal in whom the graces shine,
Lovely as summer, juvenile as spring,
Artless as nature, and a winsome thing,
Who scatter'd bliss where'er her footsteps trod,
And communed secretly in prayer to God !

The curious villagers in favours white,
Flock'd to the church to see the wedding sight ;
To scatter flowers and dazzle her with smiles,
As she pass'd through the porch and crowded aisles ;
Where breathless expectation reigns within,
As groups of relatives and friends pour in.

A string of bridesmaids at the entrance wait,
In flowery garlands and in bridal state ;
While a loud peal of music from those bells
In jocund numbers the glad tidings tells,
And answering echoes from the hills reply
In spiritual voices as they softly die.
The Bride now enters, by her father led,
And a sensation through the church is spread.
On his arm leaning in a lace white veil,
And satin dress embroidered, looking pale.
With wreaths of orange blossom round her head,
And a choice bouquet, which a perfume spread.
With blushing elegance she threads her way
Through the thronged avenue of friends all gay,
Attended by her maids in white, who smile
Graceful in rosy beauty up the aisle :
Straight to the altar, where she timid stands,
Th' observed of all observers, shaking hands.
With crimson blushes, which she ill could hide,
She takes her station by the bridegroom's side ;
All serious, and attentive, and subdued,
She never felt before in such a mood.
His kind and gentle manner, nervous air,
And agitation, his first love declare,

F

A grave and solemn contract to perform,
And not an empty ceremonial form ;
Binding together for the term of life,
For good or ill, a husband and a wife.
They covenant for ever to be true,
And pledge their troth to love and comfort through
Life's mazy windings, until death them part,
Each helping with devotedness of heart.
Binding th' auspicious union with a ring,
The usual matrimonial offering :
Concluding with a prayer for nuptial joy,
And worldly blessedness without alloy.

The happy pair, in Hymen's fetters bound,
Receive the hearty shake from all around,
With warm congratulation of their friends,
Which in a scene like this such interest lends ;
With the paternal blessing to express
The hopes and wishes for her happiness.
Recover'd from their novel state of mind,
And deep emotion felt by womankind,
While passing through this era of their fate,
From which their future will receive its date ;

Admiringly they read each other's face,

And rush spontaneous to the soft embrace !

Without a word they meet each other's eyes,

And feel idolatry within them rise.

The register records the wedding rite,

The bells again rejoice with all their might ;

The gay assembly gratified departs,

With fond remembrance and responding hearts ;

While all without look animate and gay,

And scores of carriages, well fill'd to-day

With youth and beauty of the blushing fair,

Whose sparkling eyes diffuse a cheerful air :

Whose taste and elegance at once display'd

Their lofty rank and fashionable grade.

The long procession drove off to the Hall,

To breakfast at the sumptuous festival,

And toast their warmest wishes in champagne,

To the all happy pair and bridal train.

The old hall rang with long and loud hurrahs,

Long after the unveiling of the stars,

While mirth and song invoked the early dawn,

And graceful dancing welcomed in the morn.

HELICON,

𝔄 Poetical Reberie.

I.

LET pictured dreams of fancy rise
To some bright palace in the skies,
While I the magic curtain raise,
And sing elysian Richmond's praise ;
From its heaven-exalted hill,
Rising o'er yon wind-worked mill,
Where the forest's vernal bed
Invites the Sun to rest his head,
As sinking he descends the sky,
In robes of crimson imagery.
Lo ! by yonder wood of oak,
How spirally curls the smoke,

As to the clouds its volumes rise,

In fleecy drapery o'er the skies.

Ascend beyond the vapoury Earth,

Forgetting that it gave you birth,

Let elevated scenes inspire,

And bid all nether things retire.

II.

Behold Eden from this hill,

And its teeming bosom fill

With the rainbow's liveried flowers,

Fruitful vines and trelliced bowers.

What a rich luxurious scene,

In their liveries of green !

Here the lilac droops its head,

And perfumes around are spread

By the fragrant eglantine,

Hawthorn, violet, jessamine,

Gold laburnum, blushing rose,

And each tinted flower that blows,

Whose sweet breath travels hill and dale,

In the amorous sportive gale :

The sonorous minstrels in the trees

With music load the fanning breeze.

Yon avenue, down dell and glade,
From scorching sun provides a shade.
Through this garden rich and wide,
How the fairy waters glide !
Like veins of silver they appear
In the earth meandering clear,
Sweetly warbling on their way
In symphonies their plaintive lay,
As the verdant banks they lave
With the undulating wave.

III.

Here the graceful Muses dwell,
And the sounds of music swell ;
Here the nine celestial daughters
Frolic in these limpid waters.
Hill of Helicon, inspire
With enthusiastic fire !
Transport me from this lower world,
Let wings of fancy be unfurl'd,
Seal up my worldly thoughts and mind,
And loose my soul into the wind,
Where it may rove the ether field
Of Heaven, from mortal view conceal'd,

Where nought is seen but is sublime,
And youth is ever joyous,—time
Ever young,—rolling on a wheel,
The hidden future to reveal,
Lit with a luminary clear,
Without the change of Seasons here.

IV.

Come, thou fairest of the Nine,
Muse of Lyric! on me shine
Melpomene! and with thy lyre
Awake my soul and it inspire.
In yonder consecrated spot,
Almost by the world forgot,
Honour'd by the Muses' bower,
Behind yon hoary-headed tower,
By a bard's immortal name,*
This the 'Temple of his Fame,'
Dedicated to the Muse,
For a vision I would choose ;
While the rippling flowing stream,
Music weaves into my dream ;
And the Naiads raise the song,
As they leap and float along

* Pope's Villa.

The sylvan Thames, whose dulcet voice
Inspires the woodlands to rejoice ;
Which the fawns and nymphs seclude
In their rural solitude,
Where the voice of melody
Unbars the silence of the sky,
When the evening vespers bring
Minstrel birds their lays to sing,
In the fir and cedar trees,
Bowing to the amorous breeze,
Ere they sleep the night away
In their cottages of clay ;
Giving utterance to their joy,
And happiness without alloy :
Then anon, when night wanes deep,
And half the world 's entranced in sleep,
When the azure glittering sky,
With the moon of Earth slung high,
Fills the arch of Heaven's wide gate,
With its family of state,
The planets travelling round the Sun,
Or at his heels like chase begun ;
Then the melody is heard
Of that little tenor bird

Sweet Philomel ! chantress of night,
Rapturous, plaintive, exquisite ;
Full, loud, and clear, while all is mute,
Her soft notes. sweet as Lydian flute,
Pour down upon the verdant glade,
From out the brake or sylvan shade,
Mellifluous as the glassy brook,
Stealing through some hidden nook,
At the foot of some high mountain,
Mother of the sparkling fountain ;
River, streamlet, lake, cascade,
Leaping down the dingle's shade.

V.

All is hush'd and silence reigns
Through the heaven's and earth's domains ;
Night is journeying on her wheels,
Gentle sleep absorbs and steals,
Fast from me the world recedes,
Rivers, valleys, mountains, meads ;
The fring'd curtains of my eyes,
Close like vapours o'er the skies ;
My drowsy thoughts hie to their cells,
And peace within my bosom dwells ;

Languid, weary, thoughtless lying,
Image of the dead or dying ;
Lulled to rest in arms of sleep,
Mystic visions o'er me creep.
Seraphs of a distant sphere,
Watch me as I slumber here,
While my spirit nimbly flies
Up the archway of the skies !
   Journeying on expanded wing,
Aëriel shapes around me cling ;
Angel spirits from above,
Heralds from Almighty Jove ;
With their spiritual beams of light,
Robed in pure and spotless white,
Hang in folds and festoons round,
In girdles delicately bound :
Evanescent, shadowy, dim,
Resembling in form and limb
Those we knew of mortal birth
Who had passed away from earth,
Friends and dear ones whom to know,
Form'd a paradise below ;
O'er whose memory for years
We have pined and wept our tears.

VI.

Beyond the ridge of atmosphere,
Where all is open, blue and clear.
Through a maze of worlds we flew,
Now unfolded to our view ;
And my soul by instinct led,
Through the pleiades made head
To the central milky way,
Radiant with the eyes of day ;
Where systems into systems run,
And endless space seems just begun ;
While other nebula beyond,
Disclosed infinity around.
So up the mountain as you rise,
The circling hills increase in size,
And follow as you upward go,
Till lost in rising mists below :
While you the snowy summit climb,
Absorb'd in reveries sublime !
Communion holding with the vast
Endless creations of the past !
    Kindred spirits from afar,
Met and sprighted to a star,
Famed by bards of every clime,
Where Parnassus sits sublime ;

Where Apollo strikes his lyre,
And the faithful band inspire!
Mellifluous sounds break on the ear,
And all th' ethereal atmosphere
Is fill'd with soft euphonious strains
And vocal melodies: the plains
Of heaven awake, inspire and raise
The soul to ecstacy and praise,
Filling it with touching lays;
While harp and lute their chords supply
To fill the air with harmony;
Recalling back our elfin prime,
When passing through the porch of Time,
And sweet forgotten airs we sung
In social circles with the young.

The music of this heavenly sphere,
Like sirens' voices on the ear,
Absorbs with its whole influence
All dreamy thought and nervous sense;
When put into mesmeric sleep,
Spell-bound, charmed, and buried deep;
In the mystic chains that bind,
Every impulse of the mind;
Which has placid grown and calm,
As by some balsamic charm,

Narcotic drug, or incensed air,
Transporting us to regions where
Enchanting fairy landscapes rise,
And new creations meet our eyes !

VII.

Visionary scenes appear,
Dulcet sounds fall on the ear,
Whispering voices softly fall,
Distant echoes seem to call ;
Ethereal figures flit before,
And surround a column'd door,
With flights of steps to the façade,
As in pillar'd Temples laid ;
Partially reveal'd to view,
As their shades came issuing through ;
Forms of symmetry and grace,
With intelligence of face ;
Which bespoke them of the blest,
Active in their place of rest,
Winging to some distant sphere,
In whose beams they disappear,
Aërial messengers who fly,
And range the firmament on high ,

Some with garlands round their brow
Of the choicest flowers that grow,
Lily, rose, peach, violet,
With woodbine and sweet mignonette,
Orange and syringa bloom,
Each emitting its perfume:
Some with crowns whose lustre shed
Rays of glory round their head;
Some with lute, guitar, and lyre,
Some with torch-light to inspire:
All alive and spiritual seem,
Group'd in my pictorial dream,

VIII.

Around the portico there stand
Giant figures in command,
Draped in flowing tunics white,
Strong in armour, fierce of sight,
Who their martial trumpets blew
When we first appeared in view,
Looking with inquiring eyes,
All confounded with surprise,
Upon one in mortal guise,
Whom they challenge!—drawn in line,
They demanded pass or sign,

Masonic-like then withdrew,
And allow'd us entrance through.

Pillar'd portico we pass'd,
Corridors and galleries vast,
Into groves and shrubberies,
Winding walks and terraces ;
O'er which climb the clasping vine,
Strawberries, melons, luscious pine :
Where clumps and park-like scenery
Rejoice in all their witchery ;
Where the babbling streams are tost
Over rocks,—in glens are lost :
Leaping down the gulf in falls
Of crystal foam through fissured walls,
Into fragments split and torn,
And by drip of ages worn,
Leading to the sheltering wood,
Which invites to solitude.
Clear and bright the balmy air,
Floating in those regions fair,
Pictured landscapes swelling rise,
Like magic to admiring eyes :
In the midst were trellised bowers,
Covered o'er with creeping flowers,

Scenting every breeze that blows :
In recesses there arose
Emblems to the great of name,
Who had won immortal fame ;
Statues of the sacred Nine,
All transparent, look'd divine.

IX.

Through these retired Elysian fields,
Each opening bud an incense yields,
Of grateful odoriferous sweets,
Which it imparts to all it meets ;
Embalming every breath of air,
And scenting the whole atmosphere.
A nursery of blooming flowers,
Exhaled their fragrance after showers,
And luscious fruits threw out their scent,
While spice fields their aroma lent.
  In these shadowy regions wide,
With my Mentor at my side,
Curiously I took my way
The interior to survey,
Down the vista's opening glade,
To the ancient cedars' shade ;

Where bananas, plantains, palms,
And mammoths threw their giant arms ;
Where day's mirror, screen'd from sight,
Shed a dim cathedral light ;
Where the cool refreshing breeze,
Softly whispering in the trees,
Broke the silence of the skies,
In sweet touching melodies.
Waking up from light repose,
Slumbering ghosts of bards arose ;
Some in still retreats to walk :
Others met and seemed to talk,
Or in groups assembled round,
List'ning to some sage renown'd :
Meditative some withdrew,
Others courted public view,
Affable and social grown,
Genial spirits like our own.

　　Shadows of the great arise,
Whom we slowly recognise,
Shapes of disembodied men
Long forgot, appeared again !
As in life familiar known,
Each had features of his own,

G

Which the spiritual of sight,
Beaming with a glow-worm's light,
By inspired perception knew,
Instantly they came in view.
Pale and spectral was their mien,
Skeletons of what they'd been ;
Outlines of their mortal state,
Vital and immaculate.
Each a character distinct,
Preserved by natural instinct,
As if Nature, while on Earth,
Stamp'd its image on their birth
Immortal ! and in each soul,
Transfused a likeness of the whole,
With all the lineaments combin'd,
Reflected in the inner mind ;
Transparent like dissolving views,
All humble followers of the Muse.

X.

Some had all the airs and grace
Mirror'd in their youthful face,
Bright and cheerful as the Spring,
Full of hope and blossoming :

Gentle, gay, effeminate,
As in life they lived of late ;
While cast in a different mould,
Some look'd thoughtful, grave and old,
Bent with age and years of woe,
With deep furrows on their brow ;
Some the rays of genius shed,
And their inspirations spread :
While each had some peculiar sense,
Distinguished by intelligence,
Where we could distinctly trace
Revelations in each face,
Which bespoke the bards of name,
Registered in works of fame.
With these spirits pale and cold,
I could no communion hold.
They had faculties to know,
I was from the Earth below.
Crowds of figures passing by,
Undistinguished seem'd to fly,
Fanning the ambrosial air,
With their pinions everywhere.
Follow'd, startled, they withdrew,
Till they faded from our view.

A sensation seem'd to spread
Through these regions, for they fled
On our approach, as if sight
Of mortal beings did affright;
Who across the frontier wide,
Herald guarded side by side,
Came disguised to spy the land,
By conception mystic, grand,
And visionary, which to know,
Warm'd my spirit to a glow
Of frenzy, which did quite absorb
And wing'd me to this distant orb:
Which was fabulous believed,
Till the Muses undeceived,
And by grace permitted man
This grim spectral world to scan,
Which was thought ideal before,
As was deem'd the Stygian shore;
Where in purgatory dwell
Those of earth we knew so well,
Doing penance for their sins,
Ere their heavenly life begins.

XI.

Thus do the decrees of Fate,
Doom our souls to penal state,
Where anxiety and care
Drive to madness and despair,
In these realms of solitude,
All who were profane or lewd ;
Infidels and sons of vice,
With the slaves of avarice,
Whose debauchery and lies
Some were wont to satirize.
Wand'ring through copse recesses,
Where the linden's hair-like tresses
Fann'd th' ambrosial air and hung :
Drooping branches found a tongue
In the sighs of rustling trees,
Wafted by the whispering breeze ;
Where the birds from spray to spray,
Twitter'd, piped, and trill'd their lay.
To the pyramidal mount,
Nigh a sparkling crystal fount,
Opening to the circle round,
Where Mount Helicon we found,
On the margin of a brook,
In a sweet sequester'd nook,

Far from noise of life and sound,
Standing upon classic ground,
Which is sacred held by all
Having entry to the Hall.
Around whose site the Bards retire,
To listen to or wake the lyre,
Or join in parts the singing choir;
Whose voices elevate and raise
The soul to its Creator's praise!

XII.

Here a scene bewitch'd me quite,
Visible to mortal sight,
Overwhelming with surprise,
As the phantoms dimly rise,
By enchantment's spell and power
In a visionary hour,
When all earthly scenes are fled,
And you to the world seem dead,
In a calm oblivious sleep,
When their vigils seraphs keep.
Like the beacons of a tower,
Or warders of the midnight hour.
Smoking incense screen'd from view,
Forms which into substance grew;

Portraits of the earthly great,
Half reveal'd sat round in state
In galleries, and seemed to rise
Like a drama 'fore my eyes!
Figures draped pass'd to and fro,
From above, around, below,
To the standards where their Muse
Inspiration still infuse.
The daughters of Almighty Jove,
'Neath their banners sat above,
In official robes of state,
Lofty, dignified, and great!
With their lyres and lutes around,
And instruments of every sound.
In a semicircle wide,
Crown'd Apollo did preside
In sovereign state above the rest,
Honour'd, reverenced, and blest!
Grave, reserved Melpomene,
Was Muse of epic poetry.
While through her counterfeited face,
Bewitching eyes and natural grace,
Thalia! all her arts display'd,
Worthy of the comic maid.

Sublime Urania sits on high,
Presiding o'er Astronomy;
Terpsichore's dramatic strains
Thrill'd the life-blood in your veins,
With music which entranced you quite,
Sweet, euphonious, exquisite!
Euterpe inspired your s ul
With melody which roun l you stole,
Lulling storms and winds to rest,
Soothing the volcanic breast,
Calming the tumultuous mind,
And transporting all mankind.
Youthful Erato, who inspires
With love so many hearts and lyres;—
Sister Calliope, whose name
Fills with eloquence and flame
The martial hero's rising breast,
And orator above the rest.
Clio, the muse of history,
Represented chronology;
Recording th' events of Time.
Gifted with eloquence sublime;
And Polyhymnia, whose desires
Art, elegance, or taste inspires!

Noble Patrons! at whose birth
All was joy 'tween heaven and earth,
Angels bright and spirits fair,
Came from heaven their bliss to share,
And inspired the sacred Nine
With an influence divine,
And install'd them into place,
Guardians of the minstrel race.

XIII.

In a circling rising tier
Numerous lyric Bards appear,
Who pursued immortal fame,
But oblivion hides their name.
Some in clusters gather round
Those for eminence renown'd,
While the organ's swelling peal,
All their senses drown and steal.
There assembled at the base,
Sat the warblers of the race,
Who, all pregnant with desire,
To Parnassus' heights aspire,
Humble followers of the great
They admire and imitate !

Next the middle-class arise,
And attract our eager eyes;
We discover some of note,
Who with genius thought and wrote;
Whose imaginative mind,
With rich intellect combin'd;
And true love's inspiring theme,
Made up life's romantic dream;
These in countless numbers rose,
With bay chaplets round their brows.
　　Next to these in order sit
Souls of genius, fire, and wit;
Highest in the ranks of fame,
With a lustre round their name;
Whose creations, vast, sublime,
Link Eternity with Time.
Original, lofty, grand,
Intellectual lights they stand,
With a majesty divine,
Favourites of the tuneful Nine;
Bards the Muses did inspire,
Whom both men and gods admire:
Whom celestial honours wait,
As above they sit in state,

In the large pictorial hall,
At the Muse's festival,
There to render homage due,
And to hold communion too,
On mysterious, solemn rites,
Only understood by sprites,
Who from other planets far,
Met in this bright twinkling star!

XIV.

Chief of minstrels, king of kings,
David sits enthroned and sings
Praises to his God on high,
Accompanied with minstrelsy,
In immortal strains sublime,
Sacred held through every clime;
And invokes in fervent prayer,
Heavenly blessings everywhere.
Hark! to his symphonious lyre,
Join your voices with his choir!

There, a poet old and blind,
With his grand pictorial mind,
Like a venerable sage,
Sits triumphant on the stage:

All surround and homage pay
To the bard of Iliad's lay !
Whose descriptive pencil drew,
And embodied forth to view
Battle fields and chiefs of name,
Who at Troy won deathless fame.

   Seated on Parnassus' height,
Virgil is reveal'd to sight,
Who invoked the Epic Muse,
Homer's spirit to infuse ;
While he sketch'd the birth of Rome,
With her destinies to come !
And immortal heroes drew,
Clad in armour, forth to view !
With Arcadia's pastoral scenes,
Rural shades and village greens ;
Bleating flocks and lowing herds,
Piping shepherds, joyous birds,
And the infancy of man,
Which in eastern climes began,
When husbandry and fruits combin'd
To bless with health and peace of mind ;
Where the exciting chase inspired,
Or fishing streams and woods retired.

XV.

Patronized by all the great
And intellectual of the state,
There was one* of lyric race,
Wore a mask upon his face,
And false flattery on his tongue,
Whose wit and criticism stung
With his satire all mankind ;
Yet to lovely woman kind.
Gay and lively he'd infuse,
All the virtue of his Muse,
And morality inspire,
With a bard's poetic fire.
To reform the age and man,
Bards and satirists began
Manners false to ridicule,
And customs which the masses rule.
Juvenal, the wit, you fear,
Cold, sarcastic, and severe,
Critic, pedagogue, and fool,
Lashing all the world to school.
From him to Anacreon turn,
Th' all-amorous to discern,

* Horace.

Sweetest minstrel of the lyre,
Filling with a warm desire
All who worship at the shrine
Of beauty, and would call it 'mine'.
Free from worldly ties and care,
Anxious thought and gaunt despair,
He would charm our life away,
In a smiling summer day,
In the bower of bliss and leisure,
Filling it with rapturous pleasure.

There is Sappho by his side,
Like a blushing charming bride,
Whose coquettish looks and eyes
Cause your panting breast to rise ;
Kindling there a secret flame,
Which you cannot quench or tame,
Filling with intense desire,
Beauty only can inspire ;
Tenderness and melting love,
Heritage of heaven above !

Bion, Moschus, Musæus too,
With Pindar, Persius, are in view,
And Catullus' blushing face,
Infusing love, delight and grace ;

And he who sung the Works and Days,*
To the Gods' immortal praise,
Who brought the inner world to light,
And Earth immured in blackest night.

The author representing Love†
Was honour'd with a seat above ;
An object of admiring eyes,
For he breath'd woman's tenderest sighs,
And warm passion with a feeling,
All have felt around them stealing ;
Who metamorphosed gods and men,
And traced their race and origin.

XVI.

The grandeur of the tragic Muse,
Exalted sentiments infuse :
Colouring mind with scenes sublime
And heavenly when we upward climb,
To hold communion with the great,
Whose gifted genius could create
Th' immortal Drama ! and pourtray
Within the limit of a play,

* Hesiod.   † Ovid.

The living world from age to age,
As represented on the stage
By actors passing to and fro,
In every scene of life below.
Around the Muse of tragedy,
In all their solemn dignity,
Eschylus and Euripides,
With the sweet Attic Sophocles,
And others of the brotherhood,
In laurel wreaths around them stood;
Time honoured fathers of the stage,
Who sketch mankind in every page!

XVII.

The middle ages rear'd a few,
Of th' immortal band in view;
After the darkness that obscured
The continent, and half immured
Europe in an abyss of night,
All veil'd from oriental sight;
When like a deluge from afar,
Th' invading Goths o'erwhelmed with war.
But happier times began to dawn,
And gild with light the blushing morn,

When clouds dissolved themselves to dew
And landscapes open'd up to view,
When intellectual minds appear,
Like clust'ring stars, to light our sphere;
Whose lofty genius leads the way,
To herald in a brighter day !

There 's Dante from the shades below,
In awful majesty and show,
Fills the preternatural tomb,
With flitting ghosts in twilight gloom ;
Dim ghastly figures of the night,
In the hot glare of furnace light,
And draws their shadows as they rise,
Illustrious in spiritual guise ;
In those two suffering realms of hell,
Where souls in lingering penance dwell,
Where sighs and groans, despair and fear,
Are ever ringing in the ear.

Lo ! Petrarch in his rustic bower
In rapturous thought beguiles the hour,
And in his sentimental lays,
Pours out his soul in strains of praise,
To her the angel of his eyes,
In tenderest soliloquies.

Romantic dreams of elder times
We find in Ariosto's rhymes,
When love and innocence beguil'd
With simple manners Nature's child.

Jerusalem ! thy wars were sung
By Tasso's all-inspiring tongue ;
When Europe 'gainst the Moslem rose,
And kings went forth to meet Christ's foes,
In crusades to the Holy land,
With squires and knights in chief command ;
When chivalry, in mail attire
Of brass or steel, their passions fire.
Camoens and many more,
The gallery crowd from every shore,
With minor bards in rolls of fame,
Too multitudinous to name.

Corneille, Racine, Fontaine, Voltaire,
In social groups were gather'd there ;
Béranger, Boileau, Lamartine,
Are peering through the marble screen :
With Schiller, Klopstock, Gesner, Wieland,
Goethe, Lessing, Heine, and Uhland.
Their well known figures come in sight,
Amongst the crowd attired in white ;

While undistinguished in the shade,
The crowded mass from vision fade.
But there were shadows of the great
Poetical of elder date,
Who through the clear ethereal light,
Like statues stood reveal'd to sight !

XVIII.

Most prominent above the rest,
The Bard of Avon stood confess'd !
Who, though once a child of Earth,
Seem'd celestial in his birth.
Whose transmigration from the sky
Rais'd man to spirituality ;
For the creations of his mind,
Like rays of intellect, combin'd
To elevate, refine, inspire,
And fill with ecstacy and fire.
In dignity, and close behind,
Grave, venerable, care-worn, blind,
Sat he whose fancy sketch'd and drew
And raised up Paradise to view ;
With Adam, father of our race,
And Eve with blushes on her face ;

His magic wand threw open wide
The gates of hell and Stygian tide,
And shewed the dark receding shore,
Where rebel angels fell before.

With Druid look and streaming beard,
Old Chaucer in the midst appeared,
The father of rude English verse,
Who did before the court rehearse
Loose tales that filled it with delight,
To while away the tedious night,
In princely halls with tap'stry hung,
Which merrily with laughter rung.
His unmask'd countenance bespoke
The humorous bard who loved a joke;
Who drew the customs of his times,
With manners bluff in jingling rhymes.

Ben Jonson, Beaumont, Fletcher, Ford,
Dramatic specimens afford,
Who nature to perfection drew,
And character held up to view.

In near proximity was seen
The minstrel of the ' Faeric Queen,'
Who sung of chivalry and love,
Romance, the forest, castle, grove,

With beauteous damsels, valiant knights, .
Legends, visions, pastoral sights,
In fairy scenes with landscape round,
Young and graceful nymphs abound ;
Restoring an oblivious age
To cheer our weary pilgrimage !

XIX.

Romance and love and war excite
The inspired bard to muse and write
With rapturous feelings, and rehearse
His dreams of fancy into verse :
Whence lyrics, odes, hymns, songs, have sprung,
Like magic from the gifted tongue,
And brought our passions into play,
Irradiating with a ray
Of cheerfulness the rigid face,
And to its sweetness adding grace.
Their name is legion, every clime
Has nurseries for sons of rhyme,
In simple, modest, flowing thought,
Into numerous fashions wrought,
And primitive as patriarch days,
When troubadour sang roundelays,

And sought the ladye's woodbine bower
With sweet guitar in moonlight hour,
Or serenaded from below
Her chamber's lattice ere he'd go.
    Of such the multitude around
The central column's base were found,
Composed of all the Muses' choir,
In honour of the magnates higher,
Who through a magnifying glass
In dumb review before us pass.
But there were those when singled out,
Did not admit of wav'ring doubt,
Whose effigies before us rise,
And whom we proudly recognise,
Belonging to a later age,
Released from earthly pilgrimage !

XX.

    There 's Dryden's old scholastic face,
Whose mind in every phase you trace,
Who dramatised the world, and drew
His characters from points of view
The compass round, and on the stage
Pourtray'd the manners of his age ;

And in the bitterest satire sung
The vices of both old and young ;
Who in his fables brought to light
The saint and sinner forth to sight.

Below there stood a dwarf* in size,
Who peer'd into the sage's eyes,
With admiration, rev'rence, pride,
And him adopted for his guide,
To lash the follies of the times
In caustic words, but honied rhymes :
And in his philosophic plan,
Sketch'd out the ways of God to man !
In love, in sympathy, and woe,
His liquid metres sweetly flow,
And kindled in a woman's breast
The tenderest passions are confest ;
Till imagery and warmth combin'd
To stamp her likeness in the mind.

There's Nature's poet them among :
See Thomson ! who the Seasons sung,
And who with each returning Spring,
Doth round our life a witchery fling ;
And with his magic wand revives,
The slumbering trees and dormant lives

* Pope.

Of every song-bird in the wood,
Immured in lonely solitude;
And spreads before us every hour
In rich attire some fragrant flower.
Hope animates the frozen breast,
And gilds with light the orient east,
Filling with ecstacy the soul
And quick'ning impulse through the whole.

There's sentimental blank-verse Young,
Whose gloomy 'Night Thoughts' found a tongue,
Like Philomela in the sky,
But not so musical or high;
With Collins, Akenside, and Gray,
Watts, Prior, Falconer, and Gay,
Blair, Savage, Shenstone, Dyer, Shaw,
And Jones in spectral guise I saw,
With Beattie, who the Minstrel drew,
In humble life and genius too,
Midst sylvan scenes, where none intrude
On the recluse's solitude.

XXI.

Poor Goldsmith, musical and sweet,
Seem'd warbling at the Muses' feet,

Whose treasured gifts exalt, inspire,
The notes of his melodious lyre ;
With village scenes and customs dear
To memory, all delight to hear.
The gems of art his fancy drew
Are natural pictures to our view.
In deep dejection there sat one*
On whom the sun's rays never shone,
Secluded, melancholy, low,
He pass'd his pilgrimage below ;
A stranger to domestic ties,
With master mind to moralize
And paint the charming scenes of home,
Living by faith on joys to come.

    Of rustic birth and low degree,
Burns cheers us with his minstrelsy,
And sung along the banks of Ayr,
His amorous ditties to the fair.
His mirthful spirit would infuse
Love, joy, and pleasure in his Muse ;
His plaintive ballads melt to tears,
When sadness in his soul appears ;
A jolly son of Bacchus he,
And pet of all good company !

        * Cowper.

Another simple self-taught swain
Indulges a poetic vein,
And fills with humbleness and joy,
The poor and friendless 'Farmer's Boy;'
Who drew the seasons as they roll
Alternately from pole to pole.

Hogg, Barton, Coleridge, Crabbe and White,
Lamb, Hood, and Keats appear in sight,
With many others of renown,
And myriads to our age unknown;
All humble followers of the lyre,
To which their heaven-tuned souls aspire.

XXII.

Montgomery near to Milton stood,
Who sketch'd the ' World before the Flood,'
And fill'd his speculative rhymes
With dreams of patriarchal times,
A heaven on earth! till Adam's race
Are scattered wide and war embrace.

At sight of laureate Southey's soul,
Mysterious shadows round us roll,
Dark, unsubstantial forms of air,
Possess'd the mind while lingering there.

Wordsworth, enclosed in giant hills,
The soul with contemplation fills,
For as they stretch across the sky,
They point to an Eternity !

 The 'Wizard of the North'* appear'd,
To poetry by instinct rear'd,
In land of mountain and of flood,
Lochs, landscapes, valleys, heather, wood,
And rich in legendary lore,
Relics and scraps of clans no more :
When troubadour with harp in hand
In Spanish costume tour'd the land,
Singing traditions handed down
From sire to son, in hall and town ;
Of crusades and the holy war,
In times remote and popular ;
When heroes brave with sword and shield
March'd to the eastern battle-field !

 Amid the firmament on high,
That fills the blue ethereal sky,
A star which satellites surround,
Emerged from unknown depths profound ;
Whose genius, like a comet's blaze,
Brought nations to admire and gaze,

   * Scott.

Whose elevated cast of mind
Made him an idol of mankind,
And gifted with mesmeric sight,
To loftier regions took his flight.
Byron's creations, fancy bred,
Spring from the heart and from the head.
His restless shade pass'd in review,
But sad and sorrowful withdrew,
Encircled with an ivy crown,
Which ill became his haughty frown.

XXIII.

That mysterious flickering thing,*
Tow'ring on expanded wing,
Abstracted, sceptical, would soar
And the wide universe explore
On wings expanded : when alone
He rear'd creations of his own ;
To other regions took his flight,
Shutting this planet out of sight,
And all the pomp, wealth, pride, and show,
Of this vain-glorious world below.
His sensibilities refined
Display'd nobility of mind ;

* Shelley.

To intellectual realms akin,
He was not of the world, though in.
His ideal life pass'd as a dream
Of fancy down oblivion's stream.
In an enchanted palace lit,
His unsubstantial fairies flit,
Like apparitions of a sphere
Invisible, assembled here !

A joyous spirit, meteor bright,
And sparkling as a flash of light,
Attracts th' assembly with his rays,
Who look on with admiring gaze,
And smiles of cheerfulness impart
With thrilling rapture through the heart :
As his melodious voice ascends,
And with his lute's soft sweetness blends,
Whose brilliant images inspire
The human breast with fond desire ;
The soul transporting with delight,
And dreams of happiness in sight,
Infusing love and human bliss,
Not in romantic worlds, but this ;
And if on angels' wings you soar
To other regions, seek for Moore !

Spiritual visions floating by,

Recall the past of memory;

When the stage-scenes of life amuse

And change like dim dissolving views;

When the bright promises of joy

Exhilarate the playful boy,

And burst like morning rays of light

In opening up the world to sight;

When youth, like an unruffled stream,

Is filled with its enchanting dream,

And life a round of pleasure looks,

Through magic glass or pictured books;

When freedom, beauty, health, and love,

Descend in sunshine from above;

Until our riper years unfold

The leaves of time and manhood mould;

When we discover life is real,

And not, as we once thought, ideal,

The spell is broken, clouds o'ercast,

While Rogers' Muse revives the past!

    Whatever path of life we tread,

A watchful providence o'erhead

Illumes the noble lofty mind

With Hope! inspiring all mankind:

Its bright'ning promises decoy,
Reanimate and fill with joy
The spring-tides of the human breast,
And in repose to seek for rest.
Though ever distant we draw near
To suns that elevate and cheer ;
If disappointment clouds the hour,
Or threat'ning tempests grimly lour,
Cast down and sad, or fill'd with pain,
Hope's quick'ning sunshine smiles again :
Imagination, swift of wing,
Returns with the reviving Spring,
To cheer us with the joys of youth,
Love, wisdom, and the voice of truth.
When life's familiar scenes are o'er,
On Campbell's wings we upwards soar,
Transported to a happier shore.

XXIV.

Poetic art is not confined
To the strong masculine of mind ;
The gentler sex, by all admired,
With souls refined, and love inspired,
By the seraphic Muse is wrought
Into such ecstacies of thought,

That filled with passion it o'erflows
And burst the barriers of repose.
Of such our country boasts a store,
Whose praises have been sung of yore ;
Whose rich imagination soars,
Beyond this vapoury world of ours,
To warmer climes which upward raise
The pious soul to prayer and praise,
And in a purer, happier state
Of being, calmly contemplate
The future with a sybil's sight,
Where spiritual beings us invite.

    Encircled 'bove the lyric Muse,
A nucleus its rays diffuse,
And like a hazy light appears,
Enclosing myriads of spheres ;
Whose glowing beams were so intense,
Immured in odorous incense,
Which screen'd and hid their forms from view,
We could distinguish but a few
Feminine minstrels known to song,
Through odes and hymns amid the throng.

XXV.

There 's Scotland's Mary, veiled from sight,
Whose captivating charms delight,
The honied sweetness of whose tongue
Was like a syren's voice, which hung
Like sweetest music on the ear,
Filling with melody the air.
Painting and poetry allied,
In harmony sit side by side.
There laurel leaves in graceful rows
Environ Opie's heav'n-arch'd brows,
Beneath which fancy seems to brood,
And glowing images protrude.
There 's Taylor, Rowe, and Hannah More,
With myriads who had gone before,
Whose righteous souls had higher birth
Than the plebeian of the earth,
Who sought to purify and raise
To nobler being in their lays
The fallen Man ! and him inspire
With holy thoughts and faith's desire ;
Sisters of charity and love
Wafting our souls to heaven above !

I

Dove-like and mournful, you may trace
In Hemans piety and grace,
With all that elevates the mind,
By nature gentle and refined,
Kindling a spiritual glow within,
Extinguishing all worldly sin.
The shade of Barbauld passes by,
Devotional, retiring, shy,
Whose life was like a heaven below,
Whose mission was mankind to shew
That Virtue, Holiness, and Prayer,
Are guardian angels everywhere.
There's Landon, youngest of the choir,
Whose bass and silvery notes inspire,
And in romantic scenes delight,
Like fairy, nymph, or playful sprite,
Shadow invisible, yet near,
Belonging to some distant sphere ;
With Baillie, Bronte, Blessington,
Whose overflowing fancies run
Through songs of gladness, love and mirth,
Embracing all the joys of earth,
With the anonymous unite,
Their radiance in a stream of light ;

Diffusing blessings on mankind,
By their superior gifts of mind.
Browning, whose sympathies extend,
To all the gentler sex, a friend
Who sought to mitigate distress,
And social ills of life redress;
With many others known to song,
Content to mingle with the throng
Whose presence threw a charm and grace
Into the features of the face!

XXVI.

Reverberating music broke
Upon my slumbers; I awoke
As from a trance *in transitu*,
With this dissolving scene in view.
My senses in clairvoyant state,
Half conscious, clung to dreams which late
Look'd living pictures to the sight,
Transparent with ethereal light;
In supernatural disguise,
That dimly fade before my eyes;
Soon as Aurora opes the morn,
And the first ray illumes the dawn,

Dimming the stars of heaven's highway,
Which vanish at the break of day,
When from the farm, shrill, loud, and clear,
Is heard the crow of chanticleer.
It seems enchantment to the mind,
Impress'd with scenes just left behind,
Of supernatural life above,
With spectral ghosts upon the move.
A glimpse of what may be our state
Immortal! at some future date!
Aërial, shadowy, still, and cold,
To mortal sense and earthly mould,
A middle state of life within,
'Twixt heaven and earth,—to both akin!
A local habitation where
After a life of anxious care,
In twilight shades, the souls of men
After their death revive again;
Heirs to that Paradise beyond,
Where spiritual bliss in Heaven is found!

ABELARD TO HELOISE.

An Epistle.

My thoughts fly to thee ever and again,
Though disunited we must e'er remain ;
For chilling dews hang o'er my harass'd brain.
Ills cling to me like leeches to the blood,
And my mind's left to chew the bitter cud
Of deep reflection ;—much I could reveal,
But cannot picture half I think and feel.
In you my spirits sweet refreshment find,
To you I freely pour out all my mind :
Remembrance crowds her sails,—dwells on the past,
But, 'bove all others, you are first and last.

What dreams delirious haunt my feverish head !
Disturb my slumbers, and arouse from bed !

At this still meditative hour of night,
What shadowy visions flit before my sight!
What means this resurrection of the past,
This tide of memory that flows so fast?
Still do I breathe in these monastic cells
Of lonely solitude? my bosom swells,
And conscience plunges me in depths of woe,
And fancy pictures even you my foe;
Whilst scalding tears still from their fountains flow:
To you I will unburthen all my mind,
Speak all the sorrows in my breast confin'd;
And if you've feeling, pity my distress
For these too copious draughts of bitterness.

But can it be that Abelard's forgot,
As he's so coldly treated, and for what?
He'll not believe you are so callous grown,
Insensible to feeling as a stone:
He thinks that time sufficiently has shown
His love was grafted upon you alone;
On you his hopes were built, and every thought
In fancy's mirror with your image fraught;
The loadstone of his heart,—his earthly sun,
And counterpart! but now a cloistered nun,

Shut out the world, a pris'ner in cells
Where brooding dark-eyed Melancholy dwells.

What can assuage my sorrow, or console
My broken heart, or frenzy of my soul ?
Or stop the flowing rivulet of grief ?
To disappointment what can give relief ?
When first I saw thy countenance divine,
Love ecstasied me, and I wish'd thee mine :
I coveted thy love, and Heaven knows well
How much my thoughts on you were wont to dwell.

Condemn the silence I've preserved too long,
And censure me, the cause of all your wrong ;
Wrongs which have plunged in fathomless despair
Your spotless soul, and hung your brow with care ;
To extenuate or excuse would sure be vain,
In one who fill'd you with such mental pain.
I know not if I'm able to recite
The hurricane of ills that rush in sight,
And stem the tide of memory from pursuit ;
Yet I must not since reading yours be mute.
Tears are the offerings of a guilty mind,
Thoughts springing to the lips we cannot bind,

Conscience upbraids me, and I feel I am
Some fiend, or monster in the shape of man;
The ravisher of all thy bliss below,
Who sowed the seeds of misery and woe.
From Heaven alone you must expect relief,
For only Heaven can mitigate your grief,—
Restore your harass'd mind to calm and rest,
And hush the sorrows of your plaintive breast:
To Heaven I pray and at the altar kneel
Before my God, who knows what pangs I feel
For the poor victim of my brutal lust,
Whose matchless beauty stimulated thirst,
Who now confides, though bleeding at the core,
In the base wretch she felt she could adore.

Insulted Heaven has punish'd the foul deed,
And for my crime made every artery bleed;
My tortured soul for liberty repines,
For now it shudders and but dimly shines;
In sadness I have wept from day to day,
And thought on Heloise though far away.
Oh! could your mind but fathom half my pain
Could you behold my plunging, feverish brain,

Could I unfold all that I've felt for you
Since last we parted and we sigh'd adieu ;
If in your love, so constant and sincere,
You dropt for me one sympathetic tear,
However merited my pangs and just,
Your soul would pity and your heart would burst.
A parasite feeds on my sorrowing heart,
And like a canker gnaws that vital part ;
Yet all my misery,—all my worldly woes,
Are signal triumphs of blood-thirsty foes ;
Whose scorn and satire I must still endure,
Though from the world I flew to find a cure ;
For as the wounded lion will confine
Himself to deserts, and till death repine,
So now within these gloomy walls is cast
Your once loved husband, Abelard, at last ;
Stung by those critics who to fame aspire,
By their satirical vindictive ire,
The eyes of men are lit with fire and rage,
The world conspires to persecute my age,
And scorpion tongues, oh, Heloise ! combine
(Although they ne'er can be unlink'd with thine)
To pluck my laurels and destroy my creed,
Upbraiding with the ignominious deed :

No relatives are left,—no friends are near,
To soothe and comfort with a generous tear,—
Dissolve the fumes of my distilling brain,
Or keep my pulse from throbbing in my vein,—
Erase dejection from my brimming eye,
Or lift for me their orisons on high!

Though envy and malicious hatred spread
A thousand terrors round my guilty head,
And fiendish libels are invented still,
Inflicting misery sharpen'd but to kill;
Though all the world conspired to do me wrong,
I will extol thy virtues in my song.
My soul flies to thee, in thee finds relief
From deep dejection and poignant grief;
Thou art the beacon of my wandering mind,
Faithful, compassionate, sincere and kind;
I praised thy learning and thy gifts admired,
And from conviction thought you were inspired.
Inestimable virtues sprung to light,
And all was graceful to enraptured sight:
Your disposition was so sweet and mild,
You shewed the woman, though you look'd a child.

Your eyes beamed eloquence, your tears would flow,
And melt the hardest heart, though cold as snow ;
Your artless looks had such bewitching power,
One lovely smile would cheer the dullest hour ;
Your voice was music and your song was love,
A gentle angel from the realms above ;
So modest, virtuous, innocent, and fair,
If heaven has such I hope I may go there.
Thy fascinating charms smit every heart,
Thy spotless beauty did a joy impart ;
The crimson blushes rising in thy cheek
And tidal bosom, more than volumes speak ;
The diamond that flashed thy sparkling eye,
Shone like the iris in an April sky ;
Mellifluous music in your mellow voice
Of dulcet sweetness made all hearts rejoice :
Beneath thy melting looks was seen to swell
The struggling sigh from its sepulchral cell ;
Suspicion never entered in thy breast,
With every virtue was thy mind imprest ;
Thy hand came trembling to the first salute,
And then thy warbling voice, soft as the lute,
Play'd like an amorous zephyr in the tree,
And was more sweet and tuneful unto me ;

Thy auburn hair and ever cheering smile,
With pleasure beamed because unmixed with guile.
Thy saint-like meekness raised a generous tear,
From adamantine hearts, when you drew near :
Affection warmed thy sympathies, and there
Thy seraph loveliness shone passing fair ;
Thy genial nature inspired every tongue,
To praise those virtues all the world has sung :
With these accomplishments and luring charms
You stole my heart and leap'd into my arms ;
I saw, I loved you ;—then my thirst for fame
Was slaked in you, to my disgrace and shame ;
For thee I bade Philosophy adieu,
And in exchange for wisdom worshipped you,
On whom my bliss depended, though unwed,
And on thy magic charms my lechery fed ;
Thou wert my prey,—rebellious nature strove,
And I enjoyed the privilege of love :
That love was mutual, its short happy reign
Has filled our lives with bitterness and pain.
To be revenged your uncle hurl'd the dart
Into the fibres of my bleeding heart :
If not in name, in deed you were my wife,
Yet, like a savage beast, he sought my life.

Young, beautiful, and loving, kind, and true,
For me ! for life ! you bade the world adieu !
And buried in a convent's gloomy cells,
Where Solitude like misanthropist dwells,
Your far-famed beauty and those lustrous eyes,
Through which the sparkling soul was seen to rise :
Those fountains flowing with your briny tears,
Were sweet confessions of your tender years.
Not for devotion did your soul embrace
The binding veil which screens that lovely face ;
You sacrificed your all for love and me,
And bowed to God the reverential knee ;
My guilt, my shame compelled me then to flee ;
From Paris I withdrew to distant climes,
To find new miseries and repent my crimes ;
For insults mock'd affliction, vexed my mind,
Wreck'd every hope, and cast me to the wind
And waves of fortune, and the shafts of death ;
Yet all these ills refused to stifle breath,
Or tear my soul from prison, or unbar
The bolts of thraldom ; doom'd to live in war,
And in the midst of trouble, combat foes,
And arm my mind, yet multiply my woes :
But Heaven in vengeance pours a flood of ills
Into my vitals, and by inches kills.

Received in a Capuchin convent here,
I lead a life religiously austere ;
Where frankincense is burning day and night,
And waxen tapers shed a glimmering light ;
Where scripture subjects of the saints surround,
Where vellum manuscripts and books abound,
And moss-grown monuments bestrew the ground.

Thy portrait's (ever present to my view)
A study for the eyes that dote on you ;
How many nights bewildered have those spheres,
Gazing on it, been dripping with my tears !
That modest blushing cheek and coral lip,
From which the nectar I was wont to sip ;
That intellectual look and thoughtful brow,
That panting bosom which inspired a glow,
With clustering curls that wave around thy head,
Awoke my sleeping memory from the dead.
I now behold thee as I saw thee first,
When all the rays of youth and beauty burst
Their rapturous eloquence into my heart,
When fancy could not with thy image part ;
When brilliant thoughts and talents first gave birth
To arduous study and delightful mirth,

When Abelard, the learned and the wise,
Blazed like a comet of a larger size.

I'd not behold thee changed with grief or years,
Or like myself drown'd in a flood of tears ;
Still would I dream thee beautiful and young,
With all thy witchery around thee flung.
I'd not look on the ruins time has made
On form and visage, which, alas ! must fade ;
I would not see thee in deep mourning clad,
Thy cheek turn'd pale, thine eye downcast and sad ;
Therefore prefer the image of thy youth,
Though it be changed, nor would I cull the truth,
But build in fancy what indeed thou art,—
An idol in the temple of my heart.

The torch of day obscured the lamps of night,
Which when withdrawn burst in a blaze of light ;
The bashful moon looks through her fleecy vest,
Like a veil'd virgin o'er yon mountain's breast,
And half the world lies in mesmeric sleep ;
But I am doomed to watch alone and weep ;
As in the pagan temple, the devout
Pure vestals watch the fires that ne'er burn out.

Oft memory's tide will rise against the will,
And on the past my fancy lingers still.
When thou wert like the polar star to me,
I've wondered what a paradise could be,
When more than Heaven I loved and worshipp'd thee.

The midnight shadows round our convent wheel,
The struggling moonbeams through my lattice steal,
A solemn stillness reigns within these walls,
And nought is heard but headlong waterfalls;
Now picturing fancy fills my mental sight,
With what my trembling hand attempts to write;
My soul, disconsolate and fill'd with grief,
Turns unto thee, and hopes to find relief;
When recollection crowds into my mind,
And keen remorse, within my breast confin'd.
Rushes from its asylum to the soul,
And preys upon my life from pole to pole:
Pensive, repentant, melancholy, sad,
By heaven, I fear ere long I shall go mad;
My crimson cheek has changed to sickly pale,
My eyes once lustrous now begin to fail;
For time has printed furrows round my brow,
And made me e'en to thee seem cold as snow;

Who with diminish'd head at once resign'd
The glittering world and pleasures of mankind,
And shut thyself in cloisters, all for one
Whose crime made him a monk and you a nun ;
Who tho' affection dwells within his breast,
Loved not more warmly, it must be confess'd,
The maid who sacrificed her all for love !
Nor heeded men below, nor gods above !

The flame of passion's dazzling to the sight,
We see but darkly what is wrong or right ;
Nor care to learn with philosophic eye,
But time unravels all the mystery :
And clears as it illuminates the mind,
Which feeds on knowledge and becomes less blind :
Yet this I dare not plead in my defence,
For who would say I had not common sense !
I will not wrong the God who gave me all
That man need wish ere my degenerate fall :
His justice I dispute not, nor complain,
Yet wish to Heaven it woo'l relieve my pain :
Just recompense of guilt,—of that disgrace,
No sacrifice can sponge,—no time efface ;

K

With me it will not in oblivion sink,
'Twas dyed with blood, and will be dyed in ink;
It will descend with my polluted name,
(Which once was rising up the steep of fame)
Into futurity; the horrid crime
Will spread electrically from clime to clime;
And Abelard will hang on every tongue,
To father vices of the old and young.
Oh, God! that such a crime should brand my name,
And all the world thus memorize my shame!
Thus to reflect is madness to the soul,
And even now the furies round it prowl,
And seize me with wild joy; their frantic mirth
Shoots in my brain, like earthquakes in the earth.
Despair has harass'd my bewildered head,
And deep consumption on my vitals fed.
Compared with mortal sufferings, we find
Th' acutest pains are center'd in the mind;
Accusing conscience, like a voice within,
Rises in judgment to avenge the sin.

When first the mirror of the day appears,
Melting the dewy flow'rets into tears,

And inspired minstrels carol in the sky,
While aromatic breezes rustle by :
And the shrill trumpet of the chanticleer,
In rural echo crowds upon the ear,
The mystic spells which round my eyelids creep,
Asunder burst and rouse me from my sleep ;
When forth to matins at the accustomed hour
Bald-headed monks along the cloisters pour
Into the chapel, where each prostrate lies,
Offering their orisons up to the skies ;
And in its turn the thrifty meal is spread,
O'er which a library of books is read ;
And vellum manuscripts to us convey
The vestiges of nations pass'd away ;
With gems of lives and olden poetry,
Found in the archives of this monastery ;
Which some transcribe, decipher, and translate,
While folio shelves are trembling with their weight.
The frugal breakfast o'er, the monks promenade
The cloisters, courts, and portico's façade :
Given to retirement, from the rest I rove,
To meditate within the sylvan grove,
Or on the cliffs or glens myself seclude,
Immured from sight in lonely solitude.

This saintly house is built upon the shore,
Where the dark swelling waters foaming roar,
Beneath the tow'ring rocks they lash and lave,
Which rear their front against the yeasty wave,
That rushes like a vessel to the skies,
Then in a furious flood descending flies;
The curling billows of the plunging main
Struggle like captives with the binding chain;
While Cynthia in her robes climbs up the sky,
And showers her silvery beams into my eye,
To guide my footsteps o'er the pebbly sand,
And feast my sight with the sublime and grand;
Creative fancy multiplies to view
Alternately, and pictures something new
To chase the thoughts imprison'd in my mind,
And stagnant sorrows in my breast confin'd.
How oft have I, when night has wrapt in sleep
The zealous monks, kept vigil o'er the deep!
How oft I've wandered through the sleepless night,
And watch'd the morn unfold its glimmering light?
To sentimental spirits such as mine,
Who 're least ambitious in the world to shine,
There is a pleasure on the rocky shore,
And music in the wind and thunder's roar!

There is delight in roaming all alone,
To climb some height and fancy all our own ;
There's consolation where the dead repose,
Where weeping cypress mourns o'er human woes ;
There's heroism in the struggling boat,
Which in the raging sea is toss'd about ;
There is society in one's own mind,
Even when sorrow's in the breast confin'd.
Indulging in reflection, thoughts will soar
Beyond our solar system, and explore
What visionary minds alone can reach,
Which cannot be described by force of speech.
Thus speculatively alone I muse,
Feasting the fancy with internal views,
Until the signal from the belfry's rung,
Which summonses to matins old and young,
When all the brethren readily obey,
And each, bare-footed, humbly kneels to pray.
Here sacred worship mitigates our woe,
And makes the priory a Heaven below;
Within whose consecrated walls there dwell
The peace and harmony we love so well,
Where life's gay scenes are ever shut from view,
And Heaven and God are all that we pursue ;

Where faith and virtue constantly supply
Food for the mind, devotion for the eye ;
Where Solitude and Meditation reign,
To salve each wound and soften every pain.
E'en then thy image opens on my view,
And draws my soul from God to be with you ;
My conscience is accuser, and my mind
A mirror to the thoughts it cannot bind ;
Guilt overwhelms me,—dries up every vein,
O'erpowers, distempers, and distracts my brain,
And dreams rise in my visionary head,
As in a maniac's.   Oh ! that I were dead !
Or could forget thee like the bird its young ;
But memory's tablet has too bold a tongue,
Too strong a feeling, and too keen an eye,
And an explosive spark that will not die.

Could you but witness what for you I feel,
Though iron-hearted, and your breast were steel,
Your feelings then would like a river rise,
O'erflow their banks, and inundate your eyes.

Driven from my friends, my country, and my home,
O'er the blank deserts of the world to roam,

My pilgrimage began, and wandering far
Beneath misfortune's undulating star,
Was like Ulysses tossed on many a shore,
From Troy returning and its field of gore,
And when my mind was pregnant with despair,
I sat me down to weep, and thought there were
Some who would mourn my absence,—loss of life ;
But chief I thought on my unhappy wife :
Then burst the voluntary heaving sigh,
With tears that forced the flood-gates of my eye.
And all the horrors of an insane mind
Rush'd o'er my brain impetuous as the wind ;
Till thought crowds thought, and my delirious head,
And throbbing pulse, by darkness are o'erspread ;
And the warm tide of life begins to ebb,
Till every sense took wing, and soul with sight
Vanish'd beyond the starry realms of night ;
As when the rebel angels fell to hell,
Being is dormant, influenced with a spell ;
All motion seems suspended,—every nerve
Is seal'd in slumber, and can nought observe,
Until the spell is broken,—life has birth,
And light again reanimates the earth.
Since writing makes me fancy I'm with you,
Again my mind's thrown open to your view,

And as the vagrant thoughts steal o'er my brain,
I seize them, pen them, dream them o'er again.
They form an index to my tortured mind,
Robb'd of that peace no untried means can find,
May heaven inspire thee, speed thy feather'd pen,
And make me feel as I were born again.

Who would contented be to live alone,
When all that's worth our living for is gone?
Who would the pangs of misery endure?
Oblivion! death sleep! is the only cure!
Do not your wandering thoughts e'er fly to me?
Has your imagination cross'd the sea?
Or fertile brain grown barren like a tree?
My former joys and griefs o'erwhelm my soul,
And half my reason's gone, if not the whole:
To me life seems a diary of wrong,
The hours are tedious, and the journey long.
All had been brutes had woman never smiled,
For she taught how to love, and tamed the wild:
Man had been heartless had he lived alone,
Without one being he could call his own.

Where is your love, affection, and regard
For him whom you were wont to call your bard?

Who sang his madrigals in the still hour
Of eventide, in fragrant scented bower,
As we sat list'ning to the skylark's song,
Nor thought the golden meads or hours too long ;
Or in the shrubbery, or the sylvan grove,
You smiling listen'd to the voice of love ;
Or while meandering with the silver stream,
You imaged life and called it but a dream.
How sweet is memory of those happy times
When musically tuned the village chimes.
And whispering zephyrs with your locks would play,
While groves of minstrels charmed us on the way ;
Lit by the torch of day or horned moon,
The hours flew swiftly, and, alas ! too soon ;
How memory in absence loves to dwell,
And feast on pleasures once enjoyed so well !

How oft when link'd together have you fed
On the love-dreams of my romantic head !
Oft would your panting bosom heave a sigh,
And start the tear to your cerulean eye,
Which then would drench (as round my neck you flung
Your ivory arms, and on my bosom hung)
Your Abelard with tears, which made him look
A weeping willow hanging o'er a brook ;

How would the modest rose its fragance spread,
And droop before your gaze its blushing head !
The nightingale, sweet melodist of song,
Would hush its singing as you passed along ;
And purling streams their minstrelsy forego,
As if they knew you would not warble so ;
Such tides of eloquence flowed from thy tongue,
Such wit and sense, and fancy from it sprung,
In such a tuneful and mellifluous strain,
As would distil the clouds from any brain.
Your auburn curls like grapes in clusters grew,
And all was graceful,—elegant in you !
How oft your artist hand has carved my name,
And left some tree memorial of your flame !
How oft the zephyrs laden with your sighs,
Would wave around me, absent from your eyes ;
How oft those rivulets of grief would flow,
When from thy presence I was forced to go !
Ere I became a wanderer of the earth,
And cursed the hour that ever gave me birth !

My blighted hopes and comfortless despair
Have so defaced me, that I'd almost swear,

To look upon me with a lynx's eye.

You would at once your Abelard deny :

So changed by grief the coinage of his face,

You'd think it was a counterfeit and base ;

So pale with anguish, and so ghostly thin,

With sunken eyeballs, and beard streaming chin,

Projecting forehead, with a dim lit eye,—

And hermit semblance, that you'd pass him by ;

For time has pilfered him of every grace,

And sorrow clouded his once cheerful face.

Although I once possessed a robust frame,

Your dubious eyes, however bright their flame,

Would fail to recognize me as the same ;

So like a living skeleton I've grown,

Skin barely mantles my transparent bone ;

The ruddy tint that blossom'd on my face,

And smile of health, the birthright of my race,

Though eagle-eyed, you would no longer trace.

The weary traveller pitch'd his tent at last,

And his sole wish is to forget the past ;

For pious friends have let the exile in,

And now he tastes monastic sweets again.

Heavenly asylum ! teach me how to die !
Thou art the passage to eternity !
Redeeming Abbot ! who dost condescend
To shield from danger, and to love as friend,
An alien on whose brow a wintry gloom
Has settled and prepared him for the tomb ;
Ye saintly friars ! whom religion guides,
And o'er whose spirits God himself presides,
Bear witness of my penitence and zeal,
As prostrate I before the altar kneel,
To pour out all my soul in earnest prayer,
And humbly worship Him who loves to spare ;
Whose tides of mercy in abundance rise,
Swift as the meteors through the azure skies :—
" Almighty Father ! by whose grace we live
And share the blessings thou art pleased to give,
In mercy ever lend thy willing ear,
To one poor wretch who holds himself sincere :
'Tis not to praise or publish what thou art
That I submit the offerings of my heart,
Lord of Creation ! Majesty Divine !
The heavens, the earth, the universe are thine !
Thee to imagine, with exalted mind
And fathom mystery, proves that we are blind :

Shall worms of dust presume to trumpet praise ?
Can they thy glory or thy wisdom raise ?
Nature's exalted works and heaven attest
Thy mightiness ! in them thou art confest.
From the beginning to the end of time,
In soul and matter, and through every clime !
Implant, oh ! God, thy precepts in my mind,
With wisdom light it, and with girders bind ;
Teach me the follies of mankind to shun,
Enter my soul and let thy will be done ;
Knock at my heart and show me how to live,
My present, past, and future sins forgive ;
Shower down thy mercies on my guilty head,
Thy grace and influence o'er my spirit spread ;
Redeem me from iniquity and vice,
And all earth's tempting follies that entice ;
Support and strengthen in affliction's hour,
When grief invades, and stormy tempests lour ;
Subdue my pride, and change my subtle heart,
Protect me ! guide me ! teach me what thou art !
Let me thy bounty and thy blessings share,
Assist, sustain, and save me from despair.
Let me to others do as I would they
Should do to me, and every good repay :

Oh! Father, I feel grateful unto thee
For all thy mercies daily shewn to me.
In thee I put my trust,—to thee I yield,
Creator! God! protect and be my shield!
Grant this petition, mitigate my woes,
Forget, forgive the malice of my foes.
Shew thy especial favour unto one,
Whose hapless lot it was to be undone
By him who prays to thee! oh! monstrous crime,
Hide it, oblivion! and entomb it, time."

I would not dictate, or presume to slight,
Now Heloise is banish'd from my sight,
I would not have her think me callous grown,
Or that my reason or affection's flown;
Too well she knows how much I felt and feel,
Than to surmise my breast is cased with steel;
If she still loves, then let her heart attend
The counsel of her Abelard and friend;—
May passion and your memory subside,
And half your thoughts at least with Heaven divide:
Look up to God!—devote yourself to Heaven!
Forget the world, and pray to be forgiven:

Salvation seek, and fix your hopes above,
From fond remembrance banish me and love ;
No longer think of him whom you lament,
Nor let your restless, yeasty mind ferment ;
Be penitent, resign'd, submissive, wise,
Exalt your thoughts, and elevate your eyes ;
Before the cross, and at the altar kneel,
Open your heart and pour out all you feel ;
Relieve your mind, unbosom all your woe,
Renounce the world, extinguish all below ;
To God be faithful, as you've been to me,
And when I pray to Heaven I'll think of thee !

Resign'd to death, and conscious that the grave,
Which grants full freedom to the meanest slave,
Alone can med'cine my disease, and free
Me from the world with which I disagree ;
One favour only have I to request,
Which to my mind surpasses all the rest ;
Affliction daily multiplies my grief,
And death alone can minister relief ;
My lamp burns dimly and my time is brief ;
I feel th' barometer of life to fall,
The tide, the pulse, the breath, I feel them all ;

This tabernacle of my soul decay !—
Transparent soon must mix with kindred clay ;
Will you, my wife and partner of my woe,
To this request your fond affection show ?—
And for my corse (so stiff, so pale and cold,—
So aged and changed, 'twould fright you to behold)
Will you,—I pray you will,—a tomb provide,
And in the Paraclete my ashes hide ?
The last sad duty ere you close your eyes
On me for ever, you will not despise,
But lift your orisons to Heaven's closed gate
(Where souls, alas ! outside will have to wait)
And Heaven implore to let the exile in,
Unbodied, changed, and purified from sin.
The tomb shall hide me until earth restore
My love-lorn Heloise, to part no more ;
Our dust shall mix,—one monument supply
Our names alone to strangers passing by !
Peace to thy soul ! for ever fare-thee-well !
Those words for ever in my bosom swell !

THE EMIGRANT'S FAREWELL.

A TIDE of thoughts flows o'er us,
  And we 're overwhelmed with sorrow ;
The open sea 's before us,
  And we spread our sails to-morrow.

To the promised land we steer,
  Through the wide but treacherous ocean,
Full of hope bedimm'd with fear,
  And with feelings of emotion.

When the sailor tempts the main,
  But one faithful heart deplores him,
And he soon returns again
  To the maiden who adores him.

But when we the anchor weigh,
  No such hope beams on our sorrow
England's white cliffs fade away,
  And her sun will set to-morrow.

I.

We have visited the ground,
  Where our dearest friends are sleeping;
We've embraced our kindred round,
  And the beautiful left weeping.

There are some to whom we're dear,
  As they sink upon their pillow,
Will remember with a tear,
  That we're on the rolling billow.

When upon a foreign shore,
  England! oft we shall regret thee;
Should we view thy face no more,
  Still we never can forget thee.

All thy struggles to be free,
  All thy fame and all thy glory,
Reigning Mistress of the sea!
  Shall e'er illustrate our story.

All thy charms we leave behind,
  Social joys and precious treasures
Will exist but in the mind,
  Source of all our future pleasures.

From the prairie wild and rude,
  Where the hostile tribes are lying,
From some dark and dreary wood,
  Where the fierce hyæna 's crying :

Shall we oft look back to thee,
  Father-land of many nations,
As we sit beneath the tree,
  Thinking of our dear relations.

Time will pass us to the tomb,
  By our children's tears attended,
Others will arise and bloom,
  Boasting from thee they 've descended.

VERSES FOR AN ALBUM.

———

The May-Bee on expanded wings,
Transports himself from home and sings
His way through fields where flowers invite
The wandering gleaner to alight;
He sips their sweets, but growing wild,
They please not this capricious child;
Who led by instinct, wing-spread flies
To nursery scenes 'neath milder skies:
Where Flora's loveliest children bloom,
And all the liquid air perfume;
While liveried in the rainbow's hues,
They smile through tears of silver dews.

These draw the immigrant from high
To beds where perfumed flow'rets lie,

Who lighting on their budding lips,
Their fragrant breath of nectar sips ;
Extracting food for winter store,
When fields and gardens bloom no more.

Thus have I wandered like the Bee,
Amid the flowers of poesy,
And cull'd from nurseries rich and rare,
These infant blossoms of the air ;
As taste or fancy might admire,
Or patron Muses did inspire :
My rambles have been unconfin'd,
Gath'ring these fragments of the mind ;
And other climes have tribute paid,
And tasteful garlands lent their aid ;
For this collection of the muse,
Deck'd with varieties of hues
Of rival look and graceful size,
The offspring of harmonious skies.

These orphans are of kindred breed,
Whose parents long have run to seed ;
And dropp'd them in the ground to bloom,
Early to find oblivion's tomb.

But Providence's all-seeing eye
Beheld them from the pitying sky,
And filled my breast with sympathy;
And then my heart with feeling beat,
They looked so fair, and smelt so sweet!
Methought I heard their plaintive sighs
In whisp'ring gales around me rise;
Who could such moving prayers resist?
I like a tender mother kiss'd,
And gave them an asylum here,
T" amuse the mind, or tune the ear.

THE NURSERY OF THOUGHT.

TO MISS B.

———

There was a time, when life was in its spring,
   The buds of fancy blossom'd into rhyme,
Inspir'd by the Muses I could sing,
   And clip the pinions of old father Time ;
But creeping age is fast extinguishing
   The intellectual flashes of my prime,
When images long struggling to get through,
Into a shower burst like a volcano.

The tide of thought is filter'd thro' my brain,
   Much as a rambling current thro' the earth.
When mountain dews dissolving into rain,
   Sink into fissures, and burst into birth.
The soil 's not very fertile it is plain,
   As I'm too often subject to a dearth

Of thoughts, which grow like buds upon the tree,
When comes a blight and nips them instantly.

Oh! who can feel the spirit-stirring glow,
    Which animates and warms the poet's breast,
When the rich landscapes of his fancy grow
    In his creative mind, in liveries dress'd,
And his excited feelings ebb and flow,
    With the clear stamp of genius on them press'd?
These flowers of promise which spontaneous spring,
First move the minstrel's infant lips to sing.

The noon of life, and infancy of ages,
    When not too ignorant, or o'er refin'd,
Seem the most fit and seasonable stages,
    To cultivate this garden of the mind:
We then resemble anything but sages,
    And less by heart than nature disciplin'd;
Our spirits rise like sap within the tree,
When fancy's luminous, and thoughts run free.

That few ingredients will not make a bard,
    We find out from the number who succeed;
And those who think it simple find it hard,
    In case the soil's not suited to the seed:

First, he must love, or be from birth ill-starr'd,

  Deeply reflect, and like a bookworm feed

On knowledge: have genius, mind, imagination,

And travelling store his mind with observation.

The golden age of poetry is o'er,

  And in our trading country in decline;

For neither Byron, Rogers, Scott, or Moore,

  For many seasons have composed a line.

The nation is infected more and more

  With politics and business,—so the nine

Celestial maids, forgotten, will forsake,

And leave some thousand heads and hearts to ache.

Sincerely, I am out of practice quite,

  And can't compose with much facility;

Since my familiar spirit has ta'en flight,

  My mind dismantling of sublimity:

Round it is cast the shadowy clouds of night

  Without a firmament. Ability

Is thus eclips'd and vanish'd, and my brain

As barren at the glebe without its grain.

TO ISABELLA,

ON HER EMIGRATION TO ALGOA BAY.

———

On Isabel! dear Isabel!
Whence comes this sorcerer with his spell?
Who would entice you from your home
And country, other climes to roam?

I fondly hoped 'twas all a dream,
(And would that it should still so seem)
Which o'er the surface of your brain
Rose like a bubble on the main.

But since you 've foster'd and caress'd,
And hugg'd the image to your breast,
And fain will quit your native shore,
Which haply you may see no more;

May heaven to you protection lend!
May guardian angels you attend!
As o'er the deep your vessel rides,
'Twixt Afric's coast and England's tides!

And, when upon that distant shore,
May all you have conceiv'd and more,
Of health, contentment, pleasure, bliss,
Be found! which could not be on this.

But if your hopes should flatterers prove,
And Eden be a solitude ;
If locust clouds e'er dim the sky,
Or disappointment cause a sigh ;

A crowd of thoughts will cross your mind,
Of home and friends you've left behind ;
And you'll remember with a tear
All those who are to Memory dear !

What sweet remembrances will rise,
And pass before your musing eyes,
Of social joys and youthful days,
Lit with fair promise's bright rays !

Dear Isabel ! dear Isabel !
One last embrace, and then farewell !
May Heav'n to you its favour shew,
And angels tend you here below !

TO MISS W.

When the luminous spirit that late was so gay,
From the glare of the world and the crowd turns away;
When the beating heart rocks like a wreck on the shore
In the bosom which swells to the maid we adore;

When the language of thought may be read in the eye,
As distinctly as may the contents of the sky
Through the glass of the sage,—may the passion of love
Be clearly discern'd as the planets above.

When abstracted in thought we absent ourselves here,
And create in our minds an ethereal sphere,
There we image an angel in feminine guise,
And adore in our hearts what is fixed in our eyes,

Through the dark clouds of fear that encompass
    our way,
Breaks a glimmer of hope, like the twilight of day,

That infuses a calm o'er the storm-troubled mind,
But anon leaves the shades of reflection behind.

When we lay down our head on the pillow to rest,
There to lull in soft slumbers our heart-heaving breast ;
Tho' our senses have sunk in their chambers of sleep,
Dreams arise in the brain as the waves in the deep.

The flashes of lightning,—the meteors of heav'n,
Burst out like the sparks from a flint that is riv'n :
As they pass through the regions of space they illume,
But suddenly vanish and leave us in gloom.

The feelings which struggle in a love-smitten breast,
Can no more than the thoughts of the brain be
    suppress'd,
And though we should stifle, beguile, or conceal them,
Our cheek will grow pale. and our passion reveal them.

TO MISS W.

ON A PROSPECT OF LEAVING ENGLAND.

I.

By that pearl-drop in thine eye,
By that soft heart's plaintive sigh,
And your anxious state of mind;
My heart grieves to leave behind,
One I've loved so true,—so well;
But Fate bids me say Farewell!

II.

Stem the rising of that grief,
For with you my time is brief:
Soon I leave my native shore,
I may never visit more.
Suddenly tho' thus we part,
Dearest girl! you have my heart.

III.

All I felt, and all I feel,
Mortal tongue could not reveal!
Would my thoughts were in the skies,
Read by your heav'n-piercing eyes;
Then you 'd sympathise with me,
As I cross'd the briny sea.

IV.

Think not distant climes can change,
Or from you my love estrange:
There your likeness I'll address,
And my lips your lips shall press,
As the past I back recall,
Mixing honey thus with gall.

V.

When the foaming waters roar
Round me; and the storm-clouds pour
When the winds our vessel scourge,
And she dives beneath the surge;
Think of me and shed a tear,
If I'm still to memory dear.

EPITAPH.

THE friends we held in life most dear,
Should be remember'd with a tear;
And when our souls refuse to grieve,
Imprinted in our hearts should live
The deeds by which a mother's known,
Worthy to be engraved on stone.
No vain appeal need here be given,
Her deeds are register'd in Heaven,
Where she has fix'd her blest abode,
And left us lingering on the road,
Her earthly absence to lament,
But Memory is her Monument!

EPITAPH.

———

Hush'd is the voice which oft infused delight ;
   And closed the glassy eye of light and heat ;
Inanimate the countenance once bright,
   And motionless the heart that nimbly beat.

Here lies the wreck of all we once held dear,
   A loving father and a faithful friend ;
So genial, generous, faithful, and sincere,
   That memory will preserve him to the end.

——— ———

EPITAPH.

In sound and solemn sleep he rests below,
Deaf to the world, and blind to all its woe;
Inanimate! unconscious! here he lies!
A prototype of all that lives and dies!
An evergreen shorn of its vernal bloom,
In slow consumption found an early tomb!
Remembrance will preserve and hold him dear,
While love dissolves itself into a tear.
A brother's shade still flits before our eye,
As in a mirror, 'wakening memory;
Which with a quick'ning glance the past reviews
And brings before us *him* on whom we muse,
Till fancy grows familiar with his face,
And we forget th' illimitable space
That lies between us! but his spirit free,
Flies to fulfil its future destiny!

HELVELLYN.

THE rich and smiling valley lies before,
Enclosed on either side by giant hills,
Whose frowning ridges stretch into the clouds.
A beaten track points out the alpine way
To one fixed point,—the stranger's map and guide.
And we who dare to climb the mountain's brow.
The nether leave for those exalted scenes,
The narrow for the broad, and unconfin'd !
Man's dwelling for the soaring eagle's flight !

The gently rising hill in steepness grows
As we ascend : the cottages below
Diminish as we cast our eyes around :
The landscape widens as we upward rise,
And hills immured in hills, unseen before,
Now first disclose their peaks and hoary heads !

We pause awhile, and reticent admire
The rich and verdant scenery around,
The glassy lake that in the distance looks
A shining mirror, and the rising group
Of brethren crowd around and wall us in.
Deep in the narrow vale the cattle graze,
And timid sheep look scared with wild surprise
At the strange sight of man : scarce visible,
A moving figure stalks athwart the scene,
In the retired and quiet farm below ;
And so minute that the attentive eye,
Without the aid of fancy scarce makes out
The form and outline of a crawling man.
The roar of waters down the furrow'd sides
Of the majestic mountains lends an air
Of animation to the quiet scene
That reigns above the village haunts of men ;
And if o'ertaken with the shades of night,
You in the mist are lost and hid from view,
Creates a double solitude around.
In every step lies danger ; and despair
Tempts you to sit upon the cold damp ground,
And to lie down and sleep, and wake no more.

Above, the mountain's crest conceal'd in haze,
Unfolds itself majestic'lly to view:
The clouds disperse, like flying Mercuries,
Into the fields of air, and leave serene
The sun-pierced sky, which glows upon the earth.
Like the warm crimson blush upon the cheek
Of virgin modesty! On the dim ridge,
An undistinguishable shade appears,
Which slowly creeps along the tow'ring height
Of the veil'd peak, like to a winged sail
On the broad bosom of the watery deep,
Diminished in the distance to a speck!
So moves that figure o'er the mountain's brow,
Disguis'd by distance in the gathering clouds,
Its species, tribe and sex alike unknown!

The soaring eye impels the weary foot,
As the attractive object draws us on
Insensibly, absorbing every thought!
Midway we stand aloft, and doubtless seem,
To such as view us in the distant vales,
Like moving insects of the emmet's hill.
As from the lower world we fast recede
Life's busy cares engross the worldly mind,

We breathe a bracing atmosphere above,
And feel an impulse throbbing at our breast,
The chiding voice of conscience trampling down
The swelling pride of an ungrateful heart.
The majesty of Nature, and the scene
Which opens on our mute astonish'd eye,
Reveal the power of God in his sublime
And wondrous works : these elevate the soul,
Raising it from its tabernacle state,
To that it will enjoy supremely blest,
Freed from the chains that bind us to the earth !

In front a precipice of rugged rocks,
Which pierce the storm-clouds as they sweep the sky.
Frowns angrily upon us, as we 'tempt
The dangerous track.   The loose disjointed stones,
All in confusion piled, as if a war
Of Cyclops had been waged in elder times,
Dart fierce and threat'ning looks as we approach
The narrow pass, which sends defiance down.
We face the danger and to conquest march,
Like the bold veterans to a hill-crowned fort,
Whose cannon thin the brave besiegers' ranks.
From rock to rock along the ridge we climb

With cautious step and slow the dizzy height,
In silent watchfulness and anxious fear,
Scrambling o'er heaps of loose disjointed rocks,
That tremble 'neath our footsteps: rough and strewn
The impregnable barrier chokes the way,
And stops our further progress: frustrated
In our daring enterprise we pause,
But resolution and corporeal strength
Buoy up our sinking courage; on we go
Turning and doubling like the hunted hare,
And by a desp'rate spring an outlet gain.
Another precipice waylays our route,
And high in air we swing upon our hands
Over a deep ravine; the thread of life
Now hangs upon the firmness of our grasp;
For if we lose our hold, a gulf below
Receives the mangled corses of the slain.

This difficulty master'd, danger's o'er,
And down the rocks we find an easy way,
That leads up to a steep and slippery hill,
Quite perpendicular, whose summit gain'd,
Our conquest is complete and laurels won.
Again we scale the slope with hands and feet,

And often foil'd return with vigour new,
Repeating our attempts to mount the green
And level plateau, which treach'rous to our feet
Sinks with us down the side, where prostrate lie
The weary climbers panting in the sun.
One final effort the lost ground regains,
And the wish'd point where all our labours tend,
Is crown'd with victory, for the highland's ours!

A glorious prospect opens on the sight;
The panoramic views which cheer'd the way
With glimpses of the scenery around,
Are here developed; stretch'd before us lies
Th' encircling picture of the wide domain.
Transported with the sight, we roll our eyes
In general survey, struck with mute surprise!

A family of hills around us rise,
Wild, desolate and savage, whose broad backs
And lofty summits fill the crowded sky;
And cast their shadows in the glittering lakes.
These hoary-headed monarchs of the storm,
Heap'd in confusion 'midst the general wreck,
Look like the ruins of the flooded Earth.

Communing with the vast inspires the mind,
And fills it with creation's noblest works !
Soaring from earth to heav'n contemplative,
On the swift wings of fancy : here we sit,
And humbly crouching 'fore creation's fane,
In pious notes of gratitude and praise,
Confess one sovereign Author over all !

The lovely valleys clothed in velvet green,
In the soft lap of nature find repose ;
Heaving their gentle breasts between the hills,
Encircling with their arms the sylvan scene.
Amidst the gay attire, and rural scents
Of the rich scenery that glads our sight,
The pastoral nook with its reclining flock,
All cluster'd 'neath the oak's umbrageous shade,
Invites the eye to rest in tranquil gaze,
On the sweet calm of nature's soft retreats.

O'er these aerial children of the sky,
And far beyond their wide extended chains,
Stretching upon the horizon's boundary line,
Hangs veil'd in darkness the descending storm,
That falls in flood-showers on the thirsty earth !
Near this epitome of rueful night,

In contrast mingles the resplendent day,
With all the life invigorating touch
Of cheerful animation : trees in bloom,
And graceful hanging woods float o'er the lake,
Whose limpid waves in gentle volumes roll,
Chased by the sighing gale in amorous play.
The little warbling tenants of the wood
Delight the ear with their well practised lays
Of vocal harmony in concert strains,
Tuning our hearts to melody and song.
Deck'd in their summer clothing all appear,
The hills, the vales, the woods, the flowery meads ;
And o'er them thrown an universal smile
From the glad face of Heav'n, whose kindly beams
Reanimate from winter drowsiness
The torpid earth, and all its frozen roots.
Awak'ning in the infancy of Spring
The buds and blossoms of the shooting trees,
Whose summer foliage from the sultry sun,
Affords a grateful shelter and retreat.

Exalted like a beacon in the midst
Of this imposing landscape, we revolve
And bring the shifting panorama near.

Selecting objects of deep interest,

Embracing in our view fair Scotland's hills,

And the rich scenery that between them lies

Over the joining counties : as we turn,

The Irish Channel opens on our sight !

In all the grandeur of the watery waste,

While all around the calm reflecting lakes,

Embosomed in the waving woods appear

Robed in the freshest green; the lordly hills

Majestically rise on every side,

Like solid towers of admantine strength.

Below, the fruitful fields, with hedges girt,

Wave with the golden harvest, or the bloom

Of the sweet-scented bean, and clover white,

Or yellow garlic, or the poppy red ;

With simple wild flowers creeping down the side,

With ferns and orchids of the sloping dell,

Forming a fair and varied garden scene,

Adorned with infant pines of modest growth,

And healthy evergreens, a hardy race ;

With the luxurious blossom of the trees

That have withstood the fierce attacks of time,

Through ages that have slipp'd like youth away,

Reared in the forest of a thousand years !

SONNET.

THY shade, dear 'Ellen,' hovers round us here
    In all its airy lightness,—all the grace
    And heavenly sweetness emblem'd in thy face,
As though thou wert a seraph in this sphere,
Still tuning with sweet melody the ear,
    That fondly listen'd to the Muse's lyre,
    When with thy minstrelsy thou didst inspire.
Is it remembrance makes thee reappear,
    Immortal as thou art, in spectral guise?
Flitting in fancy's mirror like a dream!
    Image of those blest spirits in the skies!
Or like a floating shadow of the stream!
    Haply thou art an angel sent to warn
    That future worlds o'er us begin to dawn!

SONNET.

———

Another swift-winged year has pass'd away,
   And stamp'd its deep impressions on the mind,
   Which pauses oft at turns to look behind ;—
Reviews the past, the phantoms of a day !
Sees all things change and hastening to decay !
   How many hopes of promise unfulfill'd !
   How many friends Death's stiff embrace has chill'd !
Can any blest with smiling fortune say,
   ' No cloud has cast its shadowy frown on me !'
The hand of Time has chronicled the page,
   The seasons roll, the hours of childhood flee,
And youth's meridian leads to time-worn age.
   Life 's but a dream ! and empires yet to come
   Will mix their ashes in the quiet tomb !

THE MOTHER.

In the bloom of youth like the Spring,
   We are cheerful and gay as the lark,
And flutter like it on the wing,
   O'er the ocean of life in our bark.

Our guardians watch over and rear,
   And shield us from storms as they rise;
When sickness invades, how the tear
   Will struggle and start from their eyes !

Who can fathom a mother's quick feeling
   For the infant that sleeps at her breast ?
Who can paint the anxiety stealing
   O'er her mind for the cherub at rest ?

How she sings o'er his musical notes,
   As she rocks him to sleep in her arms ;
And awake or asleep on him dotes,
   With her kisses and lullaby charms.

How her heart will instinctively swell,
   As the thought rushes into her mind,
That her infant may one day excel,
   And the idol may be of mankind !

What emotion will rise in her breast
   When the satchel is slung at his back,
And his aim is to rival the rest
   Of his fellows in book or attack.

If his merit should win him a prize,
   And the urchin his seniors excel,
Oh ! then how her feelings will rise,
   And how proudly her bosom will swell !

MELANCHOLY HOURS.

When those we love are loved in vain,
   Who still allow us hopes to cherish,
What gloomy thoughts distract the brain
   If e'er those still-born visions perish !

But mine have vanish'd in the air,
   For where's the vow, the pledge, the token ?
Dim visions fill me with despair,
   My peace, my heart, at once are broken.

If I had never loved so true,
   I should not feel such wretched sadness ;
My sighs, my tears had then been few,
   And I had never known this madness !

But memory feeds upon the past,
  And loads the throbbing breast with sorrow,
While o'er my mind a cloud is cast
  Which fills my aching head with horror.

The busy-peopled world to shun
  Would but increase my soul's emotion,
To calm which woman's tears have run
  Like oil upon the troubled ocean.

Oft would I wander forth alone,
  O'erlooked by all the eyes of heaven,
And fancy when the winds have blown,
  And on my lips their fragrance driven,

They were her kisses, and the sweet
  Reproaches of my absence from her :
Oh ! then I've felt my young heart beat
  To overflowing like a river.

But I can never know again
  The same impassioned thought and feeling
Which once fermented heart and brain,
  And throbb'd each pulse around me stealing.

My faults! I own them with a tear,
   And blush at every idle folly :
I feel their dead cold weight lie here
   An incubus of melancholy.

To friends 1 trust I've been sincere,
   To foes though waspish, not malicious,
To frailty I will drop a tear,
   And wish the sex were less capricious.

THE RECLUSE.

When eve unfurls her shadowy wing,
And the curfew bell is heard to ring,
I shake my misty head and fling
   My cares away ;
And get me home to chat and sing,
   Muse, read, or play.

My rustic cot is out of town,
A few short miles from where the frown
Of heaven's dark brow is pinioned down
   In night's attire ;
When man in fogs is bred and grown,
   As plants in mire.

Who would have dreamt long years ago,
When our old sires were at the plough,

That time would change our manners so,
            And thus refine ?
That desks should sweat our weary brow,
            And shops confine ?

In Lethe I myself seclude,
From slavery and the multitude,
Enclosed in sylvan solitude,
                Till fall of night ;
When slumber seals up servitude,
                And dreams delight.

In this retreat my thoughts run free,
As the life-sap in bark of tree,
Warm'd with inspiring liberty,
                And open sky ;
A new-born spirit reigns in me,
                And fancy's high !

My occupation I forget,
And turn me to some fav'rite,
In library or cabinet,
                To feast my mind ;
As studious as an anchorite,
                To groves resign'd.

Often like monastic friar,
From the circle I retire,
To elevate a little higher
   My bondaged soul ;
As sea and mountain most inspire,
   To them I stroll.

And there I wander forth alone,
Imagining the landscapes shown,
To be, oh ! flattering thought, my own,
   Above ! below !
O'er which the eye of fancy's thrown,
   With poet's glow.

Oh ! how it purifies the mind,
And clears the brain to leave behind
The smoke and dust, for mountain wind
   And clear bright air !
Where humble villagers are kind,
   And maidens fair !

The cot embraced in sweet woodbine,
Odorous rose, and jessamine

Which round about it fondly twine;
And garden wall,
With peaches hung, or clustered vine,
To tempt us all.

How graceful the laburnum flows,
How fresh the sweetbriar, lilac, rose!
They sweeten every gale that blows,
After a shower,
Which in the air a perfume throws
From every flower.

Contemplative I love to trace
The customs of the rustic race,
Th' inquiring eye,—the sun-tann'd face,
And simple air!
That pride may never them deface,
Shall be my prayer!

They're social, humble, happy, plain,
With virtue in their heart and brain,
Strangers to avarice and gain,
And crafty wit:
I wish the pure blood in their vein,
Flow'd in the cit.

'Tis pleasant on the stile to hear
The madrigals of songsters near,
While at the meadow's feet runs clear
      The purling brook ;
Where shepherds with their flocks appear,
      And prating rook.

The rural lane with hawthorn green,
The harvest field where peasants glean,
The deer-stock'd park of graceful mien.
      With winding streams ;
Thrice welcome are to all I ween,
      'Neath summer beams.

These are the spots where bosoms swell,
And ope their hearts their love to tell ;
And where retired alone might dwell
      The broken heart ;
And bid the noisy world farewell,
      Till death shall part.

How sweet to muse upon the lea,
Beneath some bower-like shady tree,

Where nought intrudes upon the ee,
   Save quavering lark ;
Weaving delicious melody
   Across the park.

How calm imbowr'd from every eye,
To hear the whispering zephyrs sigh,
Interpreting, as they pass by,
   Their warm debate !
As lying 'neath a crimson sky,
   You meditate !

Here pious thoughts sublimely flow,
The soul exalting with a glow
Of inspiration passing show,
   Grand, lofty, great !
Though mortal here, man has I trow
   A future state.

ODE TO SOLITUDE.

———

SWEET the charms of solitude,
Where no cares of life intrude ;
Where content and bliss inspire
The heaven-born bard to tune his lyre :
Shunning vice, the world, and folly
For the sweets of melancholy :
Like the nymph who shuns the day,
Or the nightingale of May,
When she springs her evening lay ;
When the moon awakes from sleep,
Smiling o'er the foaming deep,
Or where silver streamlets glide,
Through the pass and mountain side ;
In the hamlet, vale, and wood,
Or in plains where cities stood,

Where the whispering zephyrs sigh,
Like voices in th' echoing sky.
Far from town and crafty men,
In the silent copse or glen,
On the dark blue mountain's breast,
Where the dazzling sunbeams rest;
I will, when the web of night
Curtains up the ling'ring light,
Like the sage philosophize
On the planets in the skies;
On those rocks that break the sea,
Revel'ing at full liberty,
When the sun sinks down the sky
Like age into eternity.
Round about the lambkins bleat,
And the brooks meandering meet,
Where the cool spring trickling flows
From the mountains melting snows,
Where the bees, their cargoes bringing,
To their waxen cells are winging;
Where the aromatic gale
Wafts the song of nightingale,
And the garden's fragrant flowers,
Refresh'd with dews and gentle showers,

With grottos, bowers, and fountains spring,
And trees the gales are quivering.

Thus to live until I die,
Not conceal'd from mortal eye,
But forgotten by the crowd,
The gay, the vulgar, vain, and proud,
Is the fondest wish my heart
Wishes for its counterpart ;
With a genial bosom friend,
Whose philosophy would tend
To advance me in the knowledge
Others may pick up at college.

With my Muse I could retire,
Accompanied with lute and lyre,
Singing spiritual hymns of praise
In inspired seraphic lays !

TO MY MUSE.

As those who 're of a sentimental cast,
In their reflections mirror all the past,
And ponder well whate'er was in the mind
Of thought and feeling; so I look behind
With pleasure on the scenes I left with you,
And from my heart wish I could share them too:
And from the busy haunts of men retire,
To tune in woodland scenes th' Æolian lyre;
Where Nature's charms inspire the minstrel's breast,
In all the colours of the rainbow dress'd;
Where crystal skies illumine all the scene,
And the rich meadows, clothed in virgin green,
Invite the shepherd at the birth of day:
With sun-tanned face he whistles on his way,
And to the ewes lends his best pastoral care,
With fostering kindness, and with patient air:

Anon (for many rural cares his craft combine),
He labours soundly at the milching kine ;
And, lo ! industriously prepares his team,
To drive afield 'neath the sun's scorching beam.
How many envy e'en the rustic's life,
Who sees so little of the din and strife
Of crowded cities, where in legions herd
Men of all nations by ambition spurr'd !

How soothing to a spirit like my own,
That seeks retirement.— loves to be alone,
Is contemplation ! which abstracts the mind,
And launches into regions unconfin'd ;
Wafting the soul to visionary bliss,
New worlds creating in forgetting this.
Who would th' enchantment of the fancy feel,
From murky cities oft alone must steal,
And mould his mind in nature's rural school,
Midst shady bowers, and groves, and gardens cool.
Who would be rich in thought, I recommend
Some portion of his earlier time to spend
In solitude ; treasuring in his brain,
(That factory of thought,—creation's fane,)

All that a country residence can yield
Of dells and vales, of forest, flower and field,---
Ocean and mountain,—depth and height explore ;
On wings of wind let eagle fancy soar,
And penetrate where never soul before,
E'en in her boldest flight an entrance found ;
For what can a luxurious fancy bound ?
It shapes another world, and opens wide
The sentimental mind, and brings a tide
Of new created objects into light,
The soul endowing with a clairvoyant's sight.
Invention is the poet's art,—his strength
Lies rather in the quality than length :
Let what he would describe be painted well,
So that his soul shall glow, and bosom swell :
His flowing verse should all be clad I ween,
In elegant attire and graceful mien :
It is not rhyme that constitutes the bard,
(Which does the rapid flight of thoughts retard,)
Although it is the fashion of the muse
Those liquid sounds in poetry to use.
Mere honied sentences which smoothly flow
Are always musical and sweet we know:
A panorama is the poet's mind,
A very prism in it seems combin'd ;

It is a mine of wealth where beauties lie.
Like radiant diamonds in obscurity ;
Gems which alone the fancy can unfold,
And fashion into images of gold :
A warm imagination, and a heart
That can pourtray, and to the life impart
The tameless passions, in the language dress'd
Of inspiration throbbing in the breast,
Is of a mind poetical the test ;
Whose faithful pictures cause the soul to feel,
And all its quick'ning impulses reveal ;
Whose flights of fancy in the fields of air.
Absorb the mind and keeps it lingering there :
Whose depth of thought can hurl us to the skies,
Make all our feelings,—all our passions rise :
Curdle the blood with etchings of distress,
Or rouse the soul to arms when wrongs oppress ;
Delight the spirits and the senses charm;
Filling with pleasure *now*,—and *then* alarm :
Romantic dreams, and visions of the head,
Vain magical illusions round us spread,
Of cyclop, genii, fairy, goblin, faun ;
For these are by imagination drawn ;
Though not alone to fiction is confin'd
The vagrant thoughts of a poetic mind ;

Truth is a gem of estimable price,
Virtue looks fairest when opposed to vice ;
To point out each the moralist will aim,
If he seek living, or posthumous fame ;
Although the intent of verse it is confess'd,
Is to exalt the mind, and calm the breast !

———————

LAMENT OF MARY QUEEN OF SCOTS.

THE breeze is rustling o'er the lake,
  Whose bosom heaves a rippling sigh,
While o'er our boat the billows break,
  As from those castle walls I fly.
What days of sadness,—nights of pain,
  I suffered while a pris'ner there !
What thorns were struggling in my brain,
  And in my heart what wild despair !

Like the pale moon from out the clouds,
  From yonder frowning tow'rs I've fled,
To seek, disguised in sable shrouds,
  Some port for my bewildered head ;
And while thus rowing o'er the deep,
  With broken heart and pensive mind,
I still shall have more tears to weep,
  Although my chains are left behind.

The mountain wind is wild and rude,
  And spurns our boat from Scotia's shore,
And in the depths of solitude,
  A voice repeats, 'return no more' ;
Though orphan-like I'm left alone,
  With but one faithful bosom friend,
I'll not be widow to a throne,
  Whatever ills on me descend.

If lairds and chieftains still rebel,
  Nor seek my kingdom to restore,
I will for ever bid farewell
  To Scotia's isles I lov'd before ;
And speed to Britain's fairy queen,
  For help against the rebel clans,
When she'll unsheath the sword and glean
  For me my crown, and rightful lands.

PICTURE OF A MOTHER AND CHILD.

——— ———

Round her cream-coloured neck does he fondly intwine
    His snowy white arms like a necklace of pearls ;
And looks like a love-nymph or cherub divine,
    As he sleeps in her bosom half smothered in curls.

Would the dream of our infancy never depart,—
    That angelic face shine ever above us ;
And the same cheerful countenance spring from the heart,
    Oh ! then how our fond ones and dear ones would
        love us !

——— ——— ———

THE MANIAC.

There he lies, but seldom sleeps,
While the moon her watch-tow'r keeps ;
Nor does he distinguish day
Wheeling through the arch'd highway ;
But, insensible and wild,
Babbles nonsense like a child :
Now he hums a dismal tune
To the cold and horned moon,
And his bony fingers time
His mutt'ring lips to doggerel rhyme.
Mark his wildly staring eye,
Quite unconscious you are nigh ;
Now his eye-balls glaring out,
Seen in thought, and fixed in doubt ;
He suddenly starts forth in bed,
Reeking hot his feverish head ;

And fancies that he hies his dream :
(But oh ! it is a subtle scheme) ;
Whilst his keepers circling round,
Hear the mystery, and expound ;
They advise his head to rest,
And humour him with kind request ;
But he's deaf to all their prayers,
And delirious fiercely stares ;
For his throbbing head pursues
Visions strange, and phantom views :
Yet his memory seems to fail,
While his face turns deadly pale :
Boding many a struggle sad,
Soon to drive him doubly mad :
Now his smattering speech begun,
In a race of words still run :
See how savage-like he rears,
Now a Hercules appears ;
Raving loudly in his rage,
As if acting on the stage,
Though held down by manual force,
Struggling like a dying horse ;
Wearying nature,—losing life,
By exhaustive battle strife ;

Now in passionate despair.
He plucks and scatters wide his hair.
What a melancholy sight !
Now the storm is at its height !
Scarcely breathing in the chase ;
Till his strength declines apace,
And the struggle 's nearly o'er,
For his heart pants more and more :
The foam is scaling up his lips,
And his recking forehead drips ;
Now, the steam pours down his cheek,
For the fever 's left him weak,
And the lotion now is spread,
O'er the temples of his head ;
Which like a furnace smokes with heat,
Whilst the quick'ning pulses beat ;
And he loudly pants for breath,
At the very gates of death,
And his dismal groans are heard,
Like the distant lowing herd ;
'Tis a fearful ghastly sight,
That fills the soul with fear and fright,
Thus to see a maniac rave,
Like an angry foaming wave !

A FAREWELL.

———

Fare-thee-well! on whom depended
  All the bliss which I could feel,
For my flattering hopes are ended
  Since your bosom's lined with steel.
All I 've felt I ne'er can tell you,
  All my grief you must not know ;
Words of sorrow cannot melt you,
  Nor the tears which for you flow.
None can sound my depth of feeling,
  But have lov'd and fared like me,
For I feel my life-blood stealing,
  Like the sap from out the tree.
Hopes which blossom'd have been blighted,
  Where they grew now lurks despair,
And the dreams which me delighted
  Are not now what once they were.

Every trifle, every pleasure,
   All that I have left behind,
Will invade my weary leisure,
   And be mirrored in my mind.
Time and absence may estrange me,
   Since we're doom'd to meet no more,
Disappointment too may change thee,
   Love may fret thee to the core.
Friends we met, but soon we parted,
   Like a vision of the head,
But you left me broken-hearted,
   And I wish that I were dead.
Could I think thee so unfeeling,
   Or believe thy heart so cold,
And the love that wants revealing,
   Should it flame and not be told?
Long had I lived on thee thinking,
   Oft my mind would thee pourtray,
Now I feel my spirit sinking
   In its prison-house of clay.
Would that when I slept before thee
   I had never waked again ;
That these thoughts might not come o'er me,
   Nor my blood boil in my brain :

For I lov'd thee so sincerely,

Heaven itself I'd lost for thee!

If that thou hadst lov'd as dearly

Would you forfeit aught for me?

Though in faith we differ wholly,

And our tenets disagree,

If this is the reason solely,

We must part,—I must be free.

Fare-thee-well! for ever parted,

Dismal scenes around me spread:

Fare-thee-well! I'm broken-hearted,

And I would that I were dead.

THE WIDOW.

AN ELEGY.

She look'd ghastly and cold as the midnight hour,
　And as pale as the face of the dead ;
Moaning, shouting, and shrieking 'no more !' 'no more !'
　For delirium bewildered her head.

Abstracted in thought, she heav'd a deep sigh,
　Which resembled the groan of the dying,
As to heaven she cast her petitioning eye,
　And then to the earth turn'd it crying.

Her wedded companion had suddenly died,
　Which plung'd her in mournful despair :
She hung o'er his corse, and she bitterly cried,
　For her heart was deposited there.

She fasted and watch'd him by night and by day,
    'Twas a sad and a sorrowful sight
To look upon, as in the coffin he lay,
    By the oil-lamp's glimmering light.

Her kisses she press'd on his purple lip,
    And squeezed his stiff-frozen hand,
As the starting tears from her eyelids drip
    Like a shower of rain o'er the land.

She gave herself up to a life-long grief,
    And invited the death that had parted
The idol she loved, for their nuptials were brief,
    And she now felt alone broken-hearted.

'Twas a sad and distressing sight to see
    (For domestic affection endears),
As o'er him she droop'd like the cypress tree,
    And sprinkled his face with her tears.

APOSTROPHE TO A LOCK OF HAIR.

Pretty little lock of hair,
Flinging charms around the fair,
Hung in ringlets o'er the brow
Of a virgin pure as snow ;
Drooping underneath her eye,
Like thin clouds that sail the sky ;
Couldst thou tell the pains bestow'd
In the boudoir, in the mode
To adorn th' enamelled face,
And which lend'st a nymph-like grace,
Then like magic spread surprise
Through the crowd's admiring eyes ;
Then thou 'dst whisper in my ear
Tales I should not wish to hear,
How thou hadst been pull'd and twirl'd,
Cut and singed, and nightly curl'd ;

Pinned and braided, dress'd and blown,
By the zephyrs round thee thrown
Platted, comb'd, and perfum'd o'er
With th' scents of many a shore.
Deck'd with flowers which seem to shoot
From the soil where thou took'st root.
Like a spirit that doth pass
Came thy shadow in the glass.

Like driven snow on mountain's head,
Or wreath'd foam o'er billows spread,
Or the foliage round the flower,
Or the woodbine o'er the bower,
Or the ivy on the wall,
Or the zephyr's playful call,
Or the bird that wanders free
On the wings of liberty ;
Thou didst deck the laughing child,
Whose red cheeks with sunbeams smiled.
But of late thou 'st been confin'd,
Like thoughts prison'd in the mind.
Oh ! couldst thou those thoughts unfold
What a volume might be told !

Pledge of friendship, thou art mine,
I'll preserve thee in a shrine,
As a sacred relic given
By a blessed saint of heaven.
In my bosom thou shalt dwell,
For her sake I loved so well,
Who though absent flies to me
Whensoe'er I look on thee.

THE DESERT.

The wanderers of the desert knelt in prayers at early
    dawn,
And with their tents and baggage to the sandy plains
    are gone ;
The bustle and confusion, with tumultuous shouts and
    cries,
All in a foreign jargon, like a Babel rent the skies.

This oasis of the wilderness with animated life,
And grumbling laden camels, and the blusterous din
    of strife ;
The picturesque costume, and the folded turbann'd
    head,
With all the caravansary from their camping ground
    have fled.

Where they located by the stream, and oft sojourned
 before,
Remains the barren scorching land it was in days of
 yore :
The hot and sultry simoon sweeps over the fallen
 slain,
Whose bones are left as landmarks, and lie scattered
 o'er the plain.

In the place of braying asses, and the scattered tribes
 around,
Are rolling waves of sand and dust, with their deep
 and rushing sound ;
The tantalizing mirage enraptures with delight,
But just as you kneel down to drink, it vanishes from
 sight.

When Israel's rebel children from Egyptian bondage
 fled,
And in the wilderness of Shur were miraculously fed,
The liquid element of life was tapp'd from Horeb's rock,
By Moses' enchanted wand, who gave the magic shock.

Here the tinted flames of sunrise burst in a blaze of
 light,
Awakening from its slumbers the still dark drowsy
 night ;
And yon prismatic waning beams sink into twilight
 shade,
Which gradually expiring into crimson sunset fade.

When the evening dews arise and encompass them
 around,
They quicken their march forward to the well and
 camping ground ;
Where they pitch the tents by moonlight, and their
 humble meal prepare,
Then recline to hear a story, or to fall asleep in prayer.

As a relic of antiquity we venerate the East,
And with figurative emblems deck the intellectual feast :
Its sacred books and holy land have scattered wide
 its fame,
Set in a jewell'd diadem round its illustrious name.

The Arab pilgrims journey on to Mecca's holy shrine,
As the Christians to the sepulchre of holier Palestine:

The primitive old customs, and the culture of the ground,
With frugal fare and barter trade, still in the East
 are found.

The graceful flowing mantle, and venerable beard,
With their gravity of countenance have never
 disappear'd ;
Their simple life and manners, with their pastoral
 pursuits,
Are indigenous to climate and native as their fruits.

This is a land of metaphor, of poetry, and song,
Where the glowing fancy ranges, and the visionary
 belong :
Their legends, laws, traditions, are preserved and
 handed down,
With the oriental imagery all round about them thrown.

Imagination soars above, with Heaven itself in sight,
Where all is young and beautiful, felicitous and bright ;
And here the ideal fancy recreates in the sublime,
When contrasted with the finite and contracted things
 of Time.

Eternity is boundless as a mist-receding shore,

And poets cannot penetrate its regions nor explore,

If Creation were developed to the most exalted mind.

There still would be discoveries, and a Providence to
find.

———————————

THE GIPSIES' CAMP.

———

Yon fortune-telling gipsies still migrate from east to
    west,
With mules and braying donkies, all in tattered
    garments dressed ;
Here to-day, — to-morrow missing ; ubiquitous they
    seem ;
And their unsettled roving life an oriental dream.

In every sybil's feature of the dark Egyptian race,
You read the hieroglyphics of a prophesying face ;
Skill'd in the occult science of a mystery divine,
Delegated to the Priesthood and the Temple's sacred
    shrine.

Through these inducted mediums, betwixt the earth
 and heaven,
A supernatural power conceive, was to these prophets
 given ;
Who with sagacious cunning, conjure up a miracle,
And interpret the fabulous, the mythic, and the
 spiritual.

These swarthy dark-eyed wanderers, like the Hebrews,
 may be found
At all points of the compass which encircle us around ;
They pride themselves on clanship, and the pure blood
 of their race,
Which is too remote of origin for history to trace.

To these oracles of wisdom, and to altars that inspire,
You dedicate your offerings in blind faith as you inquire ;
If at your birth an omen dark loom'd in the meteor sky,
These astrologers will give you an ambiguous reply.

Like auricular confessors, they beckon you aside,
And with soft blandishments and charms induce you
 to confide :

Physiognomists by nature, your character they trace,
As they read the lines upon your palm, and gaze into
　　your face.

To their village haunts or tents the coy maiden they
　　entice,
With cabalistic word or sign, and flattering syren voice ;
Then with mesmeric influence, they hold her in a spell,
While they reveal the future and consult the oracle.

Your senses grow bewildered by the mixture of a bowl
Of herbs and smoking incense, that intoxicate the soul ;
But when the trance is broken, and returning sense to
　　gleam,
'Tis like the lingering shadow of a dim remembered
　　dream.

There are those who watch above, and our wandering
　　footsteps guide,
Who influence our actions, and o'er destiny preside,
A genius immortal, or angelic saint by grace,
Whose mem'ry we prefigure, and whose sympathy we
　　trace.

If in the lottery of life your chance turns up a prize,
Your good luck comes upon you with agreeable surprise;
But if a blank is drawn instead, and misfortune on
      you wait,
Then doubtless the weird sisters seem the arbiters of fate.

If to wealth, love or beauty, you ambitiously aspire,
Or to rank, fame or heirship, or a natural desire ;
How anxious are the feelings to consult the horoscope,
And look into the future full of promise and of hope !

SLEEP.

—

Sleep holds dominion over all,
  And consciousness suspends,
With all our senses great and small,
  And Death's resemblance lends.

The warbling brook, the hum of bees,
  The weary lull to rest ;
The incense of the murmuring breeze,
  Soothes the volcanic breast.

Conceal'd in this transparent shrine,
  A banish'd prisoner lies ;
Immortal spark of flame divine,
  Whose home is in the skies.

Oblivious to the world below,
  In darken'd realms we gaze,
Where shadows passing to and fro,
  Flash like a meteor's blaze.

The spectral visions of the night,
  That haunt the guilty mind,
Fade only with returning light,
  And broken links that bind.

Muse o'er the infant's placid sleep,
  And watch its tranquil doze;
No worldly thoughts their vigils keep,
  To wake its sweet repose.

There's not a sound where all is still,
  Falls on the slumbering ear;
Which to the heart imparts a chill,
  And fills the soul with fear.

How long and wearisome the hours,
  To those who cannot sleep,
When sore affliction o'er them lowers,
  And friends around them weep.

How overpow'ring to the slave,
　　By labour's sweat oppress'd ;
Who from the cradle to the grave
　　Recruits his strength in rest.

The opium eaters of the East
　　Inebriate the mind,
While on the deadly drug they feast,
　　A dreamy world to find.

When from a trance we wake and rise,
　　The mind's eye looks aghast ;
And contemplation in the skies,
　　A vision of the past.

When its co-partner takes to flight,
　　And snaps the mortal tie,
It leaves it in the dead of night,
　　In catacombs to lie.

THE BLIND.

A FEELING of sympathy enters the mind,
When implored to remember the wants of the blind ;
Their total privation and absence of sight,
Resemble a mine in the darkness of night.

As the sun at his birth never shone on that morn,
"Twere better for him had he never been born,
Since life is a blank without prospect to cheer,
Which cost her who bore him a pang and a tear.

The lot of his parents was humble and poor,
But endearment endeavour'd to find out a cure ;
They spent their small savings, but all was in vain,
After torture and cutting, with caustic and pain.

United benevolence placed him at school,
Where branches of learning were taught him by rule :
Through the aid of raised letters he learn'd how to read,
And the other keen senses made up for his need.

His eyeballs are veil'd in a thick skin of film,
And the morn and the eve are alike unto him ;
He turns to the east for a glimpse of the morn,
Then round to the west, but all light is withdrawn.

He cannot conceive of the blue starry sky,
Or of colours, which lend such a charm to the eye,—
Of creation above,—and the ocean below,—
Or beauty of face brighten'd into a glow.

When the last setting sun at the pole takes its flight,
And for months involves all in the shadows of night,
It throws a death gloom o'er the spirits of men,
When they doubt and despair of his rising again.

All fear is dispell'd at his welcome return,
When the faint streaks of light they begin to discern ;
But dismal and dreary's the path of the blind,
Without hope in the distance, or sunbeams to find.

Should disease, age, or chance, deprive one of sight,
After years of possession, it comes like a blight,
To cloud the sunshine of his happiness here,
Half dead to the world, and the friends he holds dear.

A language is taught to the deaf and the dumb,
By mechanical aid of the finger and thumb,
Through letters and words with their meaning assign'd,
Which are but the symbols and signs of the mind.

Alas! half the sorrows and woes of mankind,
Are obscured and eclipsed by derangement of mind;
When the furies and demons let loose from their chains,
Rave wildly and fiercely in over-taxed brains.

MONODY.

REMEMBRANCE of those who have pass'd to the skies,
Will recall them before us in spectral disguise,
As we fondly reflect on the good they did here,
And distil from our hearts all we feel in a tear.

Our nearest and dearest we treasure like gems,
As they droop in decline like flowers on weak stems;
When comes the fierce gale, like a thief in the night,
And mows down its victims infected with blight.

We miss them whom we were accustomed to greet,
By the social fireside, or path of the street,
And hear with surprise our dear friend is no more,
Because we had seen him a few days before.

We try to endear them by singing their praise,
And their mem'ry revive in short touching lays;
For anonymous gifts never blazon'd their name,
Or added a leaf to their laurels of fame.

As a tablet of memory enshrined in a book,
We muse o'er its pages as we inwardly look,
And dwell on the records of life's little wave,
In eulogy now that he 's gone to the grave.

How short are the hours, and how swift in their flight,
If we sleep undisturb'd through the length of the night,
An oblivious death, as though Time was no more!
An Eternity brief without e'er a shore!

As mists settle down on the mountain to rest,
Dissolve into rain and filtrate through its breast;
So widow and orphan will melt into tears,
When the 'salt of the earth' from the stage disappears.

To be of the world, and yet live to oneself,
Resembles a folio laid on the shelf;
Or tree that is barren and yielding no fruit,
Which we sentence to death, and pluck up by the root.

To scatter sunbeams through our path as we go,
And light up the countenance into a glow,
We should the philanthropist aim to excel,
In doing our mission and doing it well!

Oh! could I but find the philosopher's stone,
Whose magical influence as yet is unknown,
The charm I would keep like the wizard of old,
Who turn'd by its touch everything into gold.

No want or affliction should ever invade,
The world should a paradise be and ne'er fade,
The young and the beautiful never should die,
And the aged ascend to their home in the sky.

———————

MELODY.

—

The Seasons are emblems divine
   Of pictorial life upon earth,
When Childhood and Spring intertwine
   With garlands when launch'd into birth :
When blue and serene are the skies,
   Lit up by their luminous sphere,—
The sap and the spirits to rise,
   And bloom-buds begin to appear.

The Summer all lovely and gay,
   And Hope with its iris above,
Inspire like the beams of the day,
   And swell in the bosom of love ;
The perfume of flowers in the breeze,—
   The trill of the lark in the air,—
The blossom and fruit of the trees,
   Smile, brighten, and drive away care.

Q

The Autumn has ripen'd its grain,
 And Youth into mellowness grown,
The storm-clouds dissolve into rain,
 And our prime with its beauty has flown ;
The tinted leaves fade and decay,
 And in showers descend 'fore the blast,
The down of our head falls away,
 And the hour-glass running out fast.

The Winter, when robed in its snow,
 Looks picturesque in its attire,
And Age, with its lines on the brow,
 Sits musing alone by the fire ;
Short days, with the fogs, frost, and cold,—
 Blank niches of friends who are gone,
Remind us we're all growing old,
 With the shadows of Death round us thrown.

THE HAMLET.

Down in the East a gleam of blushing day
　Peers through the curtains that enfold the earth :
Softly awaking with a glimmering ray,
　The sleeping world just wakening into birth.

The winged creation join their tuneful lays
　In admiration, gratitude, and love !
Instinctively they sing their Maker's praise
　As they soar to the gates of Heaven above.

Advancing daylight animates the breast,
　And finds the penitents upon their knees,
In homage to the guardian of their rest,
　Ere they go forth to imitate the bees.

Th' industrious hives of business, commerce, trade,
    Will hence extinguish slavery and war;
Exchange the rifle for the pen and spade,
    And govern by equality of law.

If to the suburb villa you retire,
    Amuse your leisure hours and friends invite;
Read, write, and garden, let field sports inspire,
    For they invigorate you and excite.

Anxiety and care are left behind,
    With revelry, the playhouse, and the fair;
For homely comfort, ease, and peace of mind,
    Domestic happiness and frugal fare.

The calm tranquillity of country life,
    Is sweet retirement from the Babel town,
Where nests of vice and infamy are rife,
    And rank disease into its vitals grown.

All nature smiles with gladness and delight,
    The trees put on their emerald attire,
The sweetly scented flowers transport the sight,
    And vocal harmony the woods inspire.

The rich and verdant valley lies between
  The sloping meadows and the warbling brook,
Where flocks repose beneath the hawthorn screen,
  Through which the playful sunbeams laughing look.

The cheerful landscape in unruffled calm,
  Its beauteous pictures imprint on the sight,
And to th' imagination lend a charm
  Which fills the soul with rapture and delight.

Romantic scenes which elevate the soul,
  Entrance it with the joys of other days,
When images around our childhood stole,
  And fill'd with fancies our poetic lays.

The Village Church with yonder gothic tower,
  Looms in the distance like a beacon's light
That warns the vessel from the rocky shore,
  And into port directs the helm aright.

All rest from labour on the sabbath day,
  And groups are wending to the house of prayer,
In rustic costume and in colours gay,
  To worship their Creator who is there.

There is a natural instinct in the mind
  To bend our footsteps to the silent tomb,
To meditate while lingering on behind,
  And in the epitaphs to read our doom.

The old baronial Castle and the Hall
  Look like the spectral ruins of decay,
Which oft the Norman conquest will recall
  With many a siege and ambuscade affray.

The manor lord, or liberal-hearted squire
  Scatters his generous gifts on all around ;
His noble actions other hearts inspire,
  Like seed that fructifies in virgin ground.

Yon rural farmhouse looks a snug retreat,
  Surrounded by its barns and stacks of corn ;
The poultry yard with babble is replete,
  While in the distance sounds the huntsman's horn.

At times of haymaking and harvest-home,
  There's plenty of exhilarating cheer,
The homely farmer welcomes all who come
  With home-made wine and good old sparkling beer.

The pealing bells proclaim the wedding rite,
    And gladden all the faces of the young,
When bride and bridegroom issue into sight,
    With friends and relatives from whom they sprung.

The manly sports and pastimes of the thane,
    As hunting, shooting. angling, and horse-race,
Preserved and handed down to us remain,
    And illustrate the customs of our race.

By roads circuitous and hedgerow lanes,
    We come on parks adorned with mansion seats
Of wealthy landlords, and their wide domains,
    Of rustic cottages, and cool retreats.

Through mazy shrubberies that surround the lawn,
    Some nymph-like figures in the coppice stray,
Or to the trelliced bower for shelter drawn,
    They feast their minds and muse the hours away.

Domestic happiness and natural ties
    Combine to make a paradise of bliss ;
We dream of promises beyond the skies,
    But who 'd exchange for them a world like this ?

The clustering avenue of forest trees,
   Whose drooping branches form an arch above,
Afford a shelter from the sun and breeze,
   And shed a twilight through the shady grove.

The grand old monarchs of the waving wood,
   Who've stood the siege of Time from age to age,
Invite to dialogue or solitude
   The philosophic patriarchal sage.

As to the summer heat and glare of day,
   Succeed the setting sun and evening shade ;
The brilliant spirits of the young and gay,
   Like autumn liveries decline and fade.

The sun-tann'd reaper, up at early morn,
   Returns from labour to his humble cot ;
Met by his chubby rosebuds who adorn,
   And cheer him while he tills his garden plot.

What blest tranquillity when all is still !
   The cuckoo now repeats her plaintive note,
The lowing kine in streamlets drink their fill,
   And the fierce watch-dog bellows at the throat.

THE TOURNAMENT.

ALL was excitement in the King's highway,
Intent on pleasure and a holiday;
When heterogeneous vehicles throng'd by,
From gilded chariot down to cart and fly;
Fill'd with both sexes fashionably dress'd,
And the mobility in all their best;
The military tournament to view,
As to a race-course, or a camp review,
Through rural windings near a country town,
Adorn'd with landscapes to the open down;
But the equestrian healthy sylvan ride,
Abandoned now, was once our country's pride,
In which the graceful sylph-forms of the fair
With flowing costume were distinguish'd there.

Enclosed in palisades the lists were found,
T' exclude the rabble and to keep the ground;
Two openings for the combatants were barr'd,
Where men-at-arms and pursuivants kept guard;
The heralds with their trumpeters appear
At the two portals in official gear;
Two marshals kept in check the multitude,
And with their batons awed the rough and rude.

To the pavilions all in haste repair,
The knights and squires with the angelic fair;
Where hung the shields of those who challenged fight,
While banners, flags, and streamers wave in sight;
Assembled round the Prince upon the throne,
With the regalia, sceptre, mace, and crown:
The Queen of Love and Beauty sat in state
On crimson cushions, with the titled great;
Where blooming beauty was the envied prize,
And chief attraction of knight-errant eyes;
A train of pages, and young maidens fair,
In suits of green and pink were in the rear;
And now the distant clarion caught the ear,
Which summon'd the brave champions to appear.

Next in the programme, at the bugle's sound,
The vizor'd chevaliers bedeck'd the ground,
On prancing steeds caparison'd with plumes,
The knights attended with their squires and grooms;
Who greet the fair sex with polite salute,
And canter'd round the barriers with their suite;
Array'd with lance and shield in mail attire,
The flower of chivalry the fair admire.
Before the platform where the challenged stood,
The champions on their restless chargers rode,
And touch'd the challenger's emblazon'd shield,
Who with his lance and charger took the field,
Attended by his squire of less renown,
T' assist the knight if wounded or o'erthrown.

Twelve warriors engage in mortal strife
And dangerous conflict at the risk of life,
Who at a signal, eager for the fray,
Rehearse and tilt, retreat, and meet halfway,
Then plunge headforemost into the mêlée:
All in confusion mingled they retire
From this encountering skirmish to respire;
By different routes they reach'd the Royal Stand,
Made their obeisance and fought hand to hand,

Till one or other wounded, they withdrew
To canvas tents concealed from public view.
If in the struggle either is brought down,
They fence and skirmish till the other's thrown,
And then on foot renew the fierce attack,
Till one is overpowered or driven back.
A motley fool on foot with lance and shield,
Throws down the gauntlet and defies the field,
In boasting arrogance his luck to try,
Prepar'd to conquer or resolv'd to fly.

Reduced to half their numbers they withdrew,
To the appointed place of rendezvous;
A hundred measured paces on each side
The Royal Stand, the enemies divide;
When at a signal the proud chargers fly,
Like fiery meteors down the vaulted sky;
And the bold combatants with all their might,
Rush spear in hand into the deadly fight;
Against the rattling steel resounds the blow,
But does not injure or dismount the foe,
Though the collision, and the flash of fire,
Thrill'd through the nerves like an electric wire.

Repeated cheers reverberate the skies,
Follow'd by thousands of admiring eyes :
An anxious pause ensued ; once more in sight,
The rival combatants renew the fight ;
Firm in the saddle they half forward lean,
And spurr'd their steeds to this heroic scene ;
Encouraged, cheer'd, excited, and caress'd,
Intent to charge each other at the breast.
A spell-bound silence follow'd with a flash
Of vivid lightning, and a thunder crash :
The shock was withering, and the steeds recoil'd,
Lances were shiver'd, and rich armour spoil'd :
The favourite knight lay weltering on the ground,
Incased in armour with a gaping wound :
Entangled in the stirrup there he lay,
Till by his Squire and grooms convey'd away.
Cheer follow'd cheer, and loud applauses rung
With eulogistic praise from every tongue,
Scarves, handkerchiefs, and banners float the air,
In honour of the victor, who was there,
To claim the horse and armour for his prize,
As trophies of his tourney victories.

Again the trumpets sounded for the fight ;
Again the cavaliers appear in sight :

Three stalwart giants in the lists appear,
Brave, gallant gentlemen who knew not fear,
Such as romantic damsels might adore,
Arm'd cap-a-pie as in the days of yore :
A tower of strength they look'd upon the field,
Disguised in armour with engraven shield :
These casting lots, on foot the two begin,
Advance, retreat, and hedge the other in ;
Till breaking covert, like two beasts of prey,
With fierce and glaring eyeballs stand at bay ;
Then drawing nearer, close in battle strife,
With parried blows to take each other's life.
Till with the rapier, stretch'd upon the ground,
The black-mail'd Knight received his mortal wound :
Which brought the other champion from the rear,
To end the tourney with his lance or spear :
Both to the entrance of the lists retire,
From end to end, enclosed in mail attire ;
Their coursers snorted, neighed, and paw'd the ground,
Impatient at the bugle's welcome sound ;
Their high-bred instincts, graceful form, and air,
With matchless beauty were beyond compare.
With stately dignity, and graceful mien,
They wait the hoisting of the pennon green,

Then start their chargers cautiously and slow,
Their speed increasing as they onward go ;
One was distinguish'd by his steel cuirass,
The other by his corslet of rich brass ;
Impetuous, they rush with all their might,
With lance and shield, and charging to the right ;
Each grazed the other with a rattling sound,
And flew like wind along the answering ground ;
Then wheeling round renew the dual scene,
Through vizor'd grating, and half forward lean ;
Till in collision they received a shock,
Like to a vessel dash'd against a rock.
So violent the loud and stunning blow,
On casque and shield, the riders nearly throw ;
Thrust followed thrust, at each resounding stroke,
And crash on crash their lances split and broke :
Then snatching battle-axes from their belt,
Fought hand to hand, and angry thunder dealt,
Until their weapons into pieces flew :
Then from the scabbard, their short swords withdrew.
The challeng'd and the challenger drew nigh,
And with the usual courtesies defy.
This scientific art is one of skill,
To shew their faculty, and not to kill ;

A feat of arms, a spectacle and show,
Of fence and defence to ward off a blow ;
Manœuvring and strategic art combine,
More than brute force, each other to outshine.
As they engage, a general clash of steel,
Caused them to veer, and in the saddle reel ;
Which separates them for a minute's space,
Again to stand at bay, and face to face :
Again to enter in the general strife,
Striking each other at the risk of life ;
And now the battle rages warm and fierce,
And both their fancy corslets try to pierce,
When one good sword is shiver'd into twain,
And the brass Knight is number'd with the slain.
Rounds of applause burst from th' excited crowd,
And shouts and cheers continued long and loud.

Led forth in triumph to the Royal Stand,
And greeted by the noblest of the land,
Upon his charger the victorious Knight
Before the Queen of Beauty did alight,
And doff'd his casque, as he before her kneel'd,
To claim the honours of the well fought field ;

A flowery wreath to decorate his brow,
From the white hand he kiss'd with graceful bow,
Together with the rich and costly prize,
As trophies of his martial victories ;
Again the loud response and welcome cheer,
With dying strains of music greet the ear.

After the tourney, games and sports succeed,
As on the race-course, rivals try their speed ;
Bowling, football, and cricket tempt the young,
With wrestling by the firmly knit and strong ;
And feats of archery, when wing'd arrows fly,
At long range distance, into the bull's-eye :
The wily conjurer, with his magic wand,
Transforms and spiritualizes at command,
With sports and pastimes, leaps and games of chance,
And the exhilarating country dance.

THE STARS.

Suspended in the illimitable skies,
Dotted with myriads of celestial eyes,
Our planet, seen from any other sphere,
Looks girdled with a robe of atmosphere,
Whose vital influence and refreshing showers
With moistening dews revive the fading flowers,
And modifies the Sun's inspiring ray,
From cold of night, and glaring heat of day;
While sunbeams drawing vapour from the main,
Distill'd from clouds, dissolve in showers of rain.
Wafted in fancy, we the centre climb,
To view the marvels of this arch sublime;
Some form a System, circling round the Sun
Diurnally, and into Seasons run;
Revolving on its axis day and night,
Alternate darkness, with alternate light!

A breathless stillness reigns o'er all around,
Eternal! awful! solemn! and profound!
No sound or echo falls upon the ear,
But a death-sleep pervades from year to year.
A panorama floats before our eyes
Of all the clock machinery in the skies;
All govern'd by one universal law,
They gravitate and to a centre draw.
The spots upon the sun's disk caverns are,
And large enough to swallow up a star;
As if volcanos had belch'd out their fire
And left their burning embers to expire:
A million times as large as our own Earth,
But when and whence its origin and birth?
What if this source of light became extinct,
To which our planetary system's link'd?
What fearful darkness, and perpetual night,
Would seize with panic and destroy with blight!
What lamentations from the starving crowds.
Enveloped in an atmosphere of clouds!

At sunset, when the orb withdraws his rays
And slowly sinks into the western waves,

In richest colours of the rainbow's hues,
We gradually his gilded glories lose:
Retreating twilight follows in the rear,
And shadowy phantoms fill the mind with fear:
Involved in darkness,—lull'd into a doze,
All animated nature seeks repose;
While frosted Cynthia, modest, faint, and shy,
With borrow'd light illumes the spangled sky,
To take her nightly watch at close of day,
From local stations to the heaven's highway;
While influencing the action of the tides,
And with her consort, night from day divides;
Until Aurora, glimmering from afar,
Reveals her hues with steeds and chariot car.
Her worn-out craters tell of volcanos,
When earthquakes sunk, and labouring mountains rose;
If destitute of rain, fire, earth, and air,
No breathing creature could exist long there;
Its solitary silence,—dungeon gloom,
Depict a desert, or a lifeless tomb.

In this harmonious System planets rise,
To which our own is but a ball in size:

First, bright-eyed Venus with her smiling face,
Inclines to lock us in a fond embrace ;
Near to the Sun are Mercury and Mars,
Foreboding famine, fire, and bloody wars ;
Next bulky Jupiter with jets of light,
Sparkling as gems, and beautifully bright ;
And Saturn, with his moons and golden rings,
Intelligence from constellations brings ;
Remote Uranus looks a speck in size,
And Neptune but a grain to mortal eyes :
All in perpetual motion round the sun
Keep to their orbits and collision shun.
How numberless such kindred Systems rise
In the broad vault of these unfathom'd skies !

A giant telescope unveils to view
The endless stars beyond th' ethereal blue ;
Lost in the firmament of sparkling sand,
From every point of view they still expand
In zones above them infinite as Space,
And roofless heavens we can no farther trace.
Copernicus his wand of magic spun
And bade our planet travel round the sun ;

When Galileo's theory all revolved,
Sun, moon, and planets, and the problem solv'd;
For which discovery he was confin'd
To prison walls, for speaking out his mind.
With wreaths immortal crown the honour'd name
Of Newton, the illustrious heir of fame;
Discoverer of the gravitation scheme,
An intellectual, all-inspiring dream!
When Herschell's telescope first brought to light
And open'd worlds of promise to our sight;
With double stars and treble in array,
A brilliant exhibition and display;
Who mapp'd the Universe as it appears,
With all the stars seen from both hemispheres.

Divided into zodiacal signs,
We draw the heavens in latitudes and lines,
So that the raging dog-star, crab, or bear,
May be discover'd in the fields of air;
With that dim speck the pole-star for a guide,
And Orion and the pleiades, beside
The misty nebula and milky way,
With coloured stars attired in bright array;

So distant that a hundred years or more
Require their light to travel to our shore ;
Swifter than lightning flashing from the cloud,
Follow'd by rattling claps of thunder loud.

The fiery comets e'er portended ill,
And their long trains with consternation fill ;
When ignorance and superstition thrive,
In our industrious busy-working hive,
These by attraction into suns may fall,
And general conflagration seize on all.
Each on his separate mission seems to fly,
Like an electric spark across the sky ;
A grim-eyed monster from some nether sphere,
Comes like a demon to appall with fear ;
Then down the gulf takes his erratic flight
To distant realms, invisible to sight.

A shower of meteors cross the troubled sky,
And like a routed army scatter'd fly ;
Combustible with atmospheric air
They crack, explode, and dazzle with their glare.
Akin to Borealis' flitting rays,
With streams and columns burst into a blaze

Of variegated tints, and aërolites,
With ignis fatuus and corona's lights.

Preceded by a lull and death-like calm,
The air grew stifling, sultry, close and warm,
From a dense fog the blood-red Sun peep'd through,
While gathering clouds closed up those skies of blue,
The rain descended and the tempest blew ;
When suddenly a vivid flash of light
Burst through those nest-clouds and flew out of sight.
The storm increases, and the thunder's roar
Sounds like artillery from the echoing shore ;
The coloured iris with refracted rays,
Reflected by the sun breaks through the haze,
In varied tints of atmospheric hues,
Red, green, and yellow, violet, and blues.

Passing between our planet and the sun,
The shadow of an Eclipse has begun
To intercept the solar beams of light,
By the invasion of our satellite :
Immured in darkness, indistinct, and dim
A radiant halo circles round his limb.

The Earth's dark shadow stealing on apace,
Veils up the moon and hides her beaming face,
In an Eclipse which shuts her out of sight ;
Until in transit she resumes her light,
Arrayed in all the jewelry of night.

Amongst the clustering stars our orb is found,
Obscured and mixed with worlds which us surround ;
View'd at a distance 'tis minutely small,
And till discovered, dreamt not of at all.
Is yonder twinkling star fix'd in the sky,
Shining so bright and clear, a seraph's eye ?
Can any studious and enlighten'd mind
Believe these stars were purposely designed
T' illuminate our opaque globe at night,
Surrounded by those starry lamps of light ?
If peopled, who their nature can define,
Half spiritual, half human, and divine ?
Myriads of human beings may be there,
The wonders of Creation to declare.
All these inquiring thoughts enigmas seem,
And all the past a fable and a dream ;
With limited existence here below,
Fix'd on the earth we next to nothing know.

Time into eras annalists divide,
And take the past and present for their guide;
But the few thousand years they count from Man,
Compared to all Creation's but a span :
Trillions of Ages puzzle our ideas,
As comprehended by the rolling years ;
Beyond the highest star infinity,
And endless Space, lies dark Eternity.
Imagine chaos at Creation's dawn,
Ere planet, sun, or satellite was born ;
A vacuum without a ray of light,
Ethereal ! dark ! one long continuous night !

Time, distance, travel, measurement define,
But science fails to fix a boundary line,
Or to unfold the periods of their birth,
Or prove if like the elements of Earth,—
If uninhabited or not by man ?
Or when and where the Universe began ?
Have they a history of the dateless past ?
How far extending ? and how long to last ?
For unknown ages they have held their place,
And fill'd up barren spots in empty space.

Did these material forms from atoms rise,
And harden into substance in the skies?
Or generate like blight upon the tree,
Or zoophytes in coral reefs at sea?
As gas and vapoury matter round us flow,
Condensed, in time they may to solids grow;
E'en as secretions thrown off from the Sun,
A nucleus form'd of Earth and Moon begun,
Long, long before inhabited by man,
A law of Nature and Creation's plan.

From Nature up to Nature's God we rise,
And trace him in the never-ending skies;
In every planet, satellite, and star,
Distant or near, invisible and far,
The vital spirit which o'er all presides,
Impels to action, regulates and guides,
Throughout this Temple of the living God,
Ubiquitous all Space is his abode.
Mysterious! wonderful! sublime! and grand!
Rapt in amazement we can't understand.
Humbly adoring at this sacred shrine,
We feel his spiritual presence is divine:

The sovereign architect who form'd the whole,
And gave them being, is their life and soul;
Who animates the scatter'd worlds with light,
Which scientific aid reveals to sight;
Immensity confounds the dreamy mind,
And to our planet bids us be resigned.
The natural elements of earth and air,
With fire and water, are constituents there;
Furnish'd with wants peculiar unto Man,
By his Creator when the race began;
Who looks upon this temporary home
With hope and promise of a world to come!

———————————

TO A FRIEND.

Ere thou dost quit thy native land,
    An exile to a foreign shore,
Oh ! let me once more grasp thy hand,
    Which I have often shook before.

Perchance we may not meet again,
    Since ocean's shores will us divide ;
Then let us rivet friendship's chain,
    And be as once we were,—allied.

Let what has past be all forgot,—
    Forgiven by each for ever ;
And join in weaving friendship's knot,
    Which nought but death shall sever.

Misfortune has disturb'd thy rest,
   And likewise it has warr'd with me,
But I 've that rooted in my breast
   Which shall not perish but with thee.

To thee the secrets of my heart
   Were open,—and to thee alone ;
And canst thou coldly from him part
   To whom thou didst reveal thy own ?

It must not be,—the treacherous deep
   May in its bosom hide thy head,
And leave me o'er thy fate to weep,
   Till I have no more tears to shed.

That Heaven those funeral tears may spare,
   And turn thy winter into spring,
Where'er thou art, shall be my prayer,
   As long as memory has a string.

I ne'er can shut thee from my mind,
   But keep thee there as with a chain,
When thou art gone, and look behind,
   As if thou still didst here remain.

MELANCHOLY HOURS.

———

There are feelings which come o'er us
  We would willingly suppress,
When the past appears before us,
  Which has plung'd us in distress.

There are thoughts producing sadness
  In the heart and in the head,
Which depress and lead to madness,
  When expiring hope has fled.

When existence has grown weary
  With the ills which still pursue,
And the future looks as dreary,
  As the past our minds review.

There are scenes too well recorded
 In our lives to be forgot,
Truths the memory has hoarded,
 Which it nourish'd on the spot.

What can cheer the soul's dejection
 When deep disappointment low'rs?
Blighting years of fond affection
 In a few heart-rending hours?

Those are hours of deepest sorrow,
 When such dreams distract the brain;
Those are feelings which to-morrow
 Will with light revive again.

THE WOOD.

A PASTORAL.

Though worldly cares derange the mind,
 And forge their fetters round my brow,
How soothing 'tis to look behind,
 And at your feet myself to throw ;
Ye lisping children of the wood !
Ye nurseries of Solitude !

Were I to take a last farewell,
 And shun the vain world's changing skies,
Within your sylvan shades I'd dwell,
 And hide me from its jealous eyes ;
For in your groves of minstrelsy,
Live Peace, Content, and Harmony.

S

The ivy round the oak entwines,
    And locks its spreading arms above,
Just as a sleeping child reclines
    Around its mother's neck in love.
How odorous the zephyrs blow !
How cool the gushing spring below !

The twilight gleams along the brake,
    Receding with the setting sun ;
Th' expanding lily of the lake
    Sweetens the pool it swims upon ;
And through the dingle,—in the wood,
Where'er we turn dwells solitude.

At this still, solemn thinking hour,
    The mind in absence loves to dream
Of scenes we rambled in before,
    With friends who shared our fond esteem :
Who look like mariners to heaven ;
Which ever way their bark is driven.

Methinks the youthful dead should lie
    In some sequestered silent spot,
Beneath a willow's funeral sigh,
    Where blooms the sweet ' forget-me-not'.

For there the broken heart might swell,
Mourning o'er that it loved so well.

The invalid might solace find,
 As o'er the grave of some one dear,
Absorbed in thought, alone, resigned,
 She mournful stood and dropp'd a tear;
Knowing herself would early be
Lamented 'neath the willow tree.

The plaintive murmurs of the trees,
 Whose foliage obscures the sky,
Begets congenial thoughts like these,
 And fills with pensiveness the eye,
When our mercurial spirits fall,
As if we had no friend at all.

ON THE DEATH OF A YOUNG FRIEND.

Oh ! do not trespass on my grief,
   But leave me to my chamber's gloom ;
For from the tree of life a leaf
   Has dropp'd into the silent tomb.

The taper of his life burnt dim,
   And feebly in its socket shone ;
For Death had laid his hand on him,
   And o'er his path his shadow thrown.

His days were number'd ! on the wane,
   He wither'd in a slow decline :
And early finish'd his campaign,
   As haply I shall finish mine.

The Soul which late illumed his eye,
   And beamed through his transparent face,
Has vanish'd to its home on high,
   Its future spiritual dwelling-place.

He like a blooming flower of Spring,
   That sheds a perfume through the air,
Did cherfulness around him fling,
   And lighted up the brow of care.

He was a friend who won the heart,
   By his all genial air and tone,
And kept it as a counterpart
   By opening th' archives of his own.

Affection's bonds were twined round one,
   Who now on cankering sorrow feeds,
Whose chaos-mind 's without a sun,
   All mourning in her widow's weeds.

A babe, the image of his sire,
   Grew like an idol in her eyes ;
A mother's love who can acquire
   But those who share her sympathies

Alas ! they both must mourn him dead,
　Who living, was their life,—their soul :
And I with them a tear will shed,
　As on the waves of memory roll.

The nightingale her plaintive lay
　Will carol o'er his death-sound sleep ;
And pilgrims lingering on the way,
　Will read his epitaph and weep !

MELODY.

WHAT symphonies are these I hear
    With melodies that float the air?
To me celestial they appear,
    The world releasing of its care.

Aerial voices of the night
    Descend like seraphs from on high,
Invisible to mortal sight,
    With tenderest airs of sympathy.

They join in concert as they raise
    Their chants and anthems to the skies,
In ecstacies of joy and praise,
    And feel their inspirations rise.

List to the heralds of the sky,
   And tell what news the skylarks bring
As quavering on the wing they fly,
   And to their brooding nestlings sing.

The nightingale, so clear and shrill,
   Her carol sings at curfew hour,
When all is tranquil, calm, and still
   In thicket, dell, or ivy tower.

With other instruments of sound
   The harp and violin unite ;
The organ's thunder peals around,
   While lute, guitar, and horn delight.

The martial trumpet, drum, and fife
   Thrill through and animate the breast,
When marching to the battle strife,
   The courage of the foe to test.

The liquid note and drowning bass
   Reverberate the Temple's walls,
And fill with sound the empty space,
   In answering to the echo's calls.

The vocal voice is gift divine,
   And sonorously soft and sweet,
When treble, tenor, bass combine,
   Alternately in parts to meet.

The mother rocks and sings to rest
   The peevish babe who whimpering cries,
And from the fountains of her breast
   Soothes him with nature's fresh supplies.

The minstrel to his ladye love,
   Beneath her casement sings his lays,
And woos her as a turtle dove,
   By moonlight as he serenades.

From yonder nook the vesper bell
   Rings in the sisterhood to prayer,
And their seclusion seems to tell
   A holy family dwells there.

Who has not heard the tuneful chimes
   Break through the image of Death's sleep,
As sweet and musical as rhymes,
   Which alternate and measure keep?

REFLECTION.

The fairest flower that blooms in June,
　And spreads its velvet crimson wings,
So delicate and sweet at noon,
　In evening droops on slender strings,
And, scatter'd by the breeze too soon,
　　　　A perfume flings.

Dress'd in his robes the autumn sun,
　Sails gaily o'er the ocean wide,
But ere his midway course is run,
　The sable clouds confine his pride
To gloomy cloisters ;—like the nun,
　　　　Her charms to hide.

Thus life, alas! while in its prime,
   And young and beautiful its bloom,
Though faultless of a single crime,
   Is withering to an early tomb ;
Depress'd by cares in every clime,
          Death is our doom

Though health and peace we now enjoy,
   And every bliss the world can give,
Though new-fledg'd hopes our spirits buoy,
   Who knows how long he has to live ?
Disease may feed on and destroy
          This cob-web sieve.

There's not a sun we look upon,
   Although the world's great flatterer he,
But ill forebodes, and sets to some,
   In every clime of land and sea :
And oft when little thought to come,
          Death sets us free !

www.ingramcontent.com/pod-product-compliance
Lightning Source LLC
Chambersburg PA
CBHW030634030726
47497CB00006B/1783